# *The Secret of the Ruby Ring*

FAMILY ROOM

Yvonne MacGrory

# The Secret of
# the Ruby Ring

Illustrated by Terry Myler

MILKWEED EDITIONS

*For*
*Eamon, Jane, Donna, and Mark*
*— and in memory of my parents,*
*Sonny and Brigid McDyer*

Publication of *The Secret of the Ruby Ring* is made possible in part by a gift from the Lawrence M. and Elizabeth Ann O'Shaughnessy Charitable Income Trust in honor of Lawrence M. O'Shaughnessy.

Milkweed Editions, 430 First Avenue North, Suite 400, Minneapolis, MN 55401
Published in the United States in 1994 by Milkweed Editions
Originally published in 1991 by The Children's Press, Dublin, Ireland
Printed in the United States of America
98 99 00 01   10 9 8 7

Milkweed Editions is supported by the Elmer and Eleanor Andersen Foundation; Dayton Hudson Foundation for Dayton's and Target Stores; First Bank System Foundation; General Mills Foundation; Honeywell Foundation; Jerome Foundation; John S. and James L. Knight Foundation; The McKnight Foundation; Andrew W. Mellon Foundation; Minnesota State Arts Board through an appropriation by the Minnesota State Legislature; Literature and Challenge Programs of the National Endowment for the Arts; I. A. O'Shaughnessy Foundation; Piper Family Fund of the Minneapolis Foundation; Piper Jaffray Companies, Inc.; John and Beverly Rollwagen Fund; Star Tribune/Cowles Media Foundation; Surdna Foundation; James R. Thorpe Foundation; Unity Avenue Foundation; Lila Wallace-Reader's Digest Literary Publishers Marketing Development Program, funded through a grant to the Council of Literary Magazines and Small Presses; and generous individuals.

Library of Congress Cataloging-in-Publication Data

MacGrory, Yvonne.
    The secret of the ruby ring / Yvonne MacGrory ; illustrated by Terry Myler.
        p.    cm.
    "Originally published in 1991 by the Children's Press, Dublin, Ireland"—T.p. verso.
    Summary: When she makes a wish on a special ring, eleven-year-old Lucy is transported from her pampered present to a somewhat turbulent time in Ireland in 1885, where she must work as a servant for a wealthy family until she can find a way back home.
    ISBN 0-915943-88-3 (hc)—ISBN 0-915943-92-1 (pbk)
    [1. Space and time—Fiction.   2. Ireland—Fiction.]   I. Myler, Terry, ill.
II. Title
PZ7.M174Se      1994
[Fic]—dc20                                                                           93-35950
                                                                                          CIP
                                                                                          AC

# Contents

1   The Ruby Ring   7

2   Langley Castle   26

3   Elizabeth Makes a Discovery   51

4   The Sleepwalker   68

5   Nellie's Story   80

6   Echoes of the Past   94

7   A Cruel Blow   100

8   The Secret Stairs   107

9   Midnight Vigil   127

10   The Experiment   134

11   Plots   155

12   Counterplots   164

13   The Past Remembered   178

Acknowledgements   190

# 1   The Ruby Ring

'What a day!' thought Lucy to herself as she hurried through the streets of the usually picturesque town of Glenoran. A steady drizzle rained from a grey sky, and the surrounding hills were obscured by a thick mist.

'Oh, do hurry up, David,' she called impatiently to her younger brother who was sauntering along the footpath some way behind. 'We'll be soaked before we get there.'

'Coming, coming,' shouted David. He broke into a run, passed her with a whoop of delight and took a quick turn at the courthouse.

'I might have known,' groaned Lucy, tucking her escaping reddish-brown curls under her hood yet again. In irritable mood she also turned left and found David just where she had expected; heedless of the rain his face was pressed against the locked gate that led into the grounds of Glenoran Castle.

'David,' said Lucy crossly. 'We're going to be late for school.'

'Ah, Lucy, I just wanted to take a look ...'

'For goodness sake, David! It's only an old ruin, and you've seen it lots of times before.'

'I know, but I just like looking at it. Lucy, I'll bet there was an awful lot of fighting done here in the old days. It must have been great. Wish I'd lived then ...'

'If there was as much rain in Ireland in the old days as there is now, the soldiers probably spent most of their time slipping about in the mud,' said Lucy tartly. 'And talking about fighting — you'll catch it if you're not in time this morning.'

David didn't reply and the two children hurried along Main Street, each preoccupied with different thoughts.

David was seeing himself on the stone stairway in Glenoran Castle, a master swordsman, holding off all attackers.

Lucy was thinking of the summer holiday essay competition. They had handed in their entries when they had come back to school for the autumn term and Miss O'Donnell was going to tell them today who had won. She felt quite confident that she would get first place again this term. Her best friend, Noreen Doherty, had got second place last term and Lucy was very pleased for her. But *she* didn't want second place; she had to come first. School work came easily to her and she loved being able to answer the teacher's questions first. She knew that some of her classmates thought she was a show-off but Lucy shrugged off such criticisms. Was it her fault if she was better at most subjects than they were?

'Almost there now,' said Lucy thankfully as they passed St. Columbkille's Church. Luckily Miss Gillespie, the lollipop lady, was holding up the traffic and they got across the road without delay.

Inside the gates of St Ursula's, Lucy and David parted company to go to their respective classrooms. Noreen Doherty was waiting for her and the two friends made it just in time. They were both in sixth class and always sat together. Miss O'Donnell, who taught fifth and sixth class, was already there. Young, pretty, and easy to talk to, she was a great favourite with all the children.

The day seemed endless as one lesson succeeded another. Lunch was eaten in the schoolroom as the rain was still falling. But at last it was time for English.

The excited hum of voices died down when Miss O'Donnell held up her hand for silence.

'Well, girls,' she said with a smile, 'I'm sure you're all anxious to hear the results of the essay competition. You know what the first prize is,' and she held up the much-admired red-leather diary. 'But before I announce the winner and runner-up, I must congratulate you all on your efforts. The standard

was extremely high — so if you didn't win this time, please don't stop trying; it could be your turn next time. It's been a very difficult decision again this term, but after much consideration, I have decided that the first prize for best essay goes to ... Noreen Doherty ...'

Noreen gasped with delight as the class applauded loudly.

'... and the second prize goes to Lucy McLaughlin.'

Lucy sat numbly and dimly heard the class clapping. 'I didn't win,' she thought in amazement. 'I was sure I was going to win again.'

Noreen's face was wreathed in smiles as she went up to accept the red diary; Lucy could only muster a scowl and a muttered 'Thank you', as she collected her packet of felt-tipped pens.

'We won't have time to read the winning essay today, I'm afraid, but we will do so on Monday,' said Miss O'Donnell. 'Now, Noreen, would you please share out this box of sweets?'

Returning to her seat Noreen gazed in delight at the red diary. She had never had anything as nice as this before. Her family was poor — her father had now been unemployed for two years — and with four children they could afford no luxuries. Lucy, on the other hand, got lots of things which she just took for granted.

'Isn't it lovely?' she whispered to Lucy. 'I was so surprised to be the winner. I thought it would be you again this time. I know I'm not as good as you ... I never thought I'd beat you.'

She was so thrilled with her prize that she did not notice how silent Lucy had become.

As class was breaking up for the day the girls crowded around Noreen to congratulate her and get a closer look at her prize.

Unable to contain her anger any longer, Lucy burst out, 'Well, at least it's a start ... did any of you know that Noreen thinks she will become a famous writer some day?'

Noreen turned scarlet. 'Oh, Lucy,' she cried. 'How could you tell? That was our secret. I thought you were my friend.' With tear-filled eyes, she continued, 'I'll never speak to you again, Lucy McLaughlin.'

Nuala Gallagher put her arm around Noreen's shoulders and said kindly, 'Don't mind her, Noreen. She's just jealous that you got first prize. And anyway I hope you will become a writer some day.'

Without another word, Lucy crammed her books into her school-bag, and with a toss of her head marched out of the classroom. David was waiting for her at the school gates, and a glance at her scowling face told him all he needed to know about the results of the competition.

The rain had stopped at last and the sun shone weakly through a break in the clouds. Already the mist was clearing from the lower parts of the mountains. As they passed the fire station David caught a glimpse, through the open door, of the gleaming red fire-engine, but knowing it would only put Lucy into an even worse temper if he suggested stopping he hurried after her.

Main Street was busy with Friday afternoon shoppers, and the children had quite a wait at Daly's, the butchers, before a gap in the traffic allowed them to cross into Market Square.

'I'll bet you 10p that I see Dad's car first,' David called as he dodged between the parked cars in the Square.

'I hope you pay me this time — if I see it first.'

'I will, I will.' David's eyes eagerly scanned the parked cars. 'There it is,' he shouted triumphantly as he picked out their red Toyota. 'Remember my 10p when we get home.'

'Fat chance I have of forgetting,' muttered Lucy, still in an irritable mood.

The children made their second crossing to Logan's Supermarket. Sometimes they went in to have a chat with their father, who was manager there, but as Friday was such a busy day for him they went on home to their house on the outskirts of Glenoran. David ran on ahead of Lucy, not bothering to stop on the bridge today to check the height of the waters of the river Faney on the old castle walls; he was very hungry and hoped that Mum would have something ready for him.

As Lucy entered the house the smell of freshly baked apple-tart drifted towards her from the kitchen. Her mother greeted her with a smile. 'Well, who won the essay competition?'

'Noreen Doherty came first ... and I came second,' said Lucy shortly.

'Never mind, darling. I know you tried hard and it is disappointing for you. But you won last term ... and you'll probably win again next term.'

'That's no good,' Lucy yelled. 'I wanted to win this time too.'

'Come now, Lucy, you must learn to be a good loser. I'm sure Noreen worked very hard at her essay too. And she is your best friend after all, isn't she?'

'Not any more!' Lucy jumped to her feet and rushed out of the room, colliding with David who was just coming in and knocking his plate of apple-tart out of his hand. Taking no notice of David's cry of protest or of her mother's call to come back, she raced upstairs to her room and banged the door shut.

Throwing herself on her bed, she punched her pillows with clenched fists, sobbing, 'It's not fair. I should have won. I know my essay was better.'

Lucy's crying did not last long; thoughts of her forthcoming birthday kept coming to the surface. She was going to be eleven in two days' time and she had been looking forward to her party for weeks now. Mum always made a lovely cake and buns and lots of other things as well. And she did get such nice presents — even David always had some little thing for her. Dad was terrific at organising games, and even took part in some of them, much to the children's delight.

Then an awful thought struck her: 'What if Noreen wouldn't come to the party now?' She knew she had behaved rottenly to her. Noreen was shy, and Lucy had promised faithfully that she would never tell her secret to anyone. She was nothing better than a sneak and a tell-tale. It was the worst row that they had ever had.

'I'll go and see her first thing tomorrow and tell her how sorry I am,' she decided. 'I will, definitely . . .'

Having made this decision, she felt much better. Still lying on her bed her gaze wandered around her bedroom. Her mother had spent a lot of time decorating it in soft grey and pink. The pink-patterned curtains matched the duvet on the brass bed, and the pile of the pale grey carpet was deep and comfortable. In one corner of the room there was a small writing-desk and a reading-lamp, and on the wall above were the bookshelves that her father had made for her, to hold her many books and annuals. There was a long, low seat against one wall and ranged upon it were her numerous teddies and soft toys, and her much-prized collection of rag-dolls. On one side of her bed was a small wickerwork rocking-chair which

Granny McLaughlin had given her last birthday. Her mother had made a cushion cover from the leftover curtain material and it was Lucy's favourite chair.

'It really is quite a nice room,' she thought to herself. 'But I'd love a much bigger room . . . and my own bathroom would be great . . . something like the one I saw on that TV programme last week . . .'

Her gaze had come to rest on the rocking-chair and it reminded her that her grandmother was arriving this evening and would be staying for Lucy's birthday party on Sunday. She always played the piano for musical chairs and helped Lucy to wrap things for Pass the Parcel.

The heady scent of roasting chicken brought Lucy back to reality and reminded her how hungry she was; she had had nothing to eat when she came home from school. Just as she was swinging her legs off the bed there was a gentle tap on the door and her father came into the room. Paul McLaughlin was a tall man and Lucy thought he had a nice friendly face — except when he was cross of course. Taking a quiet sideways peep at him, she thought he didn't look as friendly as usual. So before he could say anything, she blurted out, 'I didn't win the competition.'

'So I heard,' he said, as he sat down on the edge of the bed.

'I behaved very badly today,' went on Lucy. 'I snapped at David. I knocked over his apple-tart — that hurt Mum. And, worst of all, I was horrible to Noreen . . .'

'And you on the verge of your eleventh birthday — practically a grown-up.' Her father smiled at the gloomy litany. 'But you came second — that's great.'

'But I wanted to win. Badly. That's why I was so upset.'

'Poor Lucy! Just think of all the times you're not going to win as you go through life. If you get so upset every time, your life won't be worth living. You'll live in a permanent black cloud. Besides, winning isn't all that important.'

'Losers always say that,' said Lucy despondently. 'I thought you and Mum wanted us to do well at school.'

'So we do. But we don't believe in this silly idea that one must be first in everything. Some of the most unpleasant people I've ever met won everything all along the line. And ended up being so arrogant and cock-sure that they had no friends.'

'No friends!' Lucy sat up. 'Wait a minute . . . why should, say, Noreen and all the girls in the class mind if I'm always first. That is, if I win fairly. That doesn't affect friendship.'

'Well, see how mad you got at Noreen. Just think of all the other girls. Always seeing you winning. They must feel pretty miserable. You've probably taken away all their confidence in their brain power.'

'Not a hope!' Lucy thought of Nuala Gallagher and how she seemed to delight in needling her. Was that why?

'Did I ever tell you the story of the computer and the monkey? No?' Lucy drew up her knees under her chin and settled down to listen; her father always knew a story to fit every situation. 'It seems they trained this monkey to play chess against a computer. The monkey was good but naturally they could programme the computer to play better. So it always won. The monkey did his best but no matter how hard he tried he always lost. So he just gave up. He sulked and wouldn't play any more. In the end they reprogrammed the computer so that the monkey won every third game. That kept up his interest.'

'I'll think of that every time I do an exam . . . and throw a few nuts to the monkeys.'

'Talking of computers, did you ever get around to reading that book I gave you last Christmas — *Simple Science,* wasn't it?'

Lucy flushed guiltily and glanced at the book which was sitting undisturbed on the shelf where she had put it after a quick run-through. 'Well, I did read some of it, but not much,' she admitted. 'I liked the section about the inventors best ... but, honestly, I'd rather write essays and read history — that's far more exciting.'

'But so is science. You need it to know how things work. Would you know how to create electricity, for instance, if you were cast away on a desert island?'

'Now, Dad, I'm never likely to be a castaway on a desert island. Not in this day and age. And I always intend to have people like electricians and plumbers and workmen around to do things for me. What's the point of cramming my brain with information I'm never likely to use?'

'Well, just remember you'll be starting science next year and it would be a help to know something about the subject.'

'That's a point. I'll start reading it again ... after my birthday.'

'Great! We can try a few simple experiments together. Now it must be nearly time to collect your grandmother. Her bus gets in about seven-thirty.'

'Good, I'm starving. By the way, Dad, are you giving me that present I want ...?'

'Parnell?' Her father put the accent on the second syllable.

'*Par*nell,' corrected Lucy.

'Isn't he a little adult for you? Wouldn't you prefer a book on someone like ... Robert Emmet?'

'Because of Mrs. O'Shea? We watched the TV series, Noreen and I. I'm not interested in *that* part of the story. But it was a very exciting time in Ireland, wasn't it?'

'The Land League, Davitt, Captain Boycott. Yes, it must have been quite an exciting time to live in.'

As he reached the door, Paul McLaughlin turned back. 'Do you think, by the way, you could be a little more patient with David?'

'Oh Dad, he can be such a pest! He's either trailing after me or he's jumping all over the place. And no matter what happens he always says, "Well, it's not my fault."' Lucy imitated her brother's voice.

'I know, Lucy,' said her father laughing. 'But boys are often a bit slower than girls at that age. He's only eight so he has a lot to learn. Maybe you could count to ten sometimes and it would help you to keep your temper.'

'More like count to a hundred . . . but I will try harder.'

As they passed by the kitchen, Lucy put her head in and said, 'Sorry about what happened earlier.'

'That's all right, Lucy. Just remember not to take it out on the apple-tart next time. All that effort slaving over a hot stove — and it ends up on the floor.'

'I'll do the wash-up after supper,' Lucy offered contritely.

'Great! Now, hurry off or you'll miss the bus. I hope it's on time or the supper will be ruined.'


Half a hour later, Paul and Lucy were back with Granny McLaughlin. There was a great flurry of hugs and kisses before things settled down.

David, who had taken charge of his grandmother's suitcase, called, 'Mum, will I take Gran's case upstairs?'

'Yes. Put it in the spare room.'

Lucy followed with two parcels that Gran had asked her to leave in her room. 'One of these must be my birthday present,' she thought. 'I wonder what it is?'

When the children came down, the grown-ups were having a glass of sherry and talking about friends and family.

'How is everything at the farm?' Jean McLaughlin was asking.

'Just fine, dear. Dick and Rosa are busy painting the bedrooms at the moment. Jim and Charlie were in a state of excitement yesterday when one of the cows had twin calves.'

Dick was Paul's elder brother and the farm was seventeen miles north of Glenoran. It was where Paul McLaughlin had been born and brought up and where Martha McLaughlin had come as a bride many long years ago. She now lived there with her son Dick, his wife Rosa, and their two children Jim and Charlie. Lucy and David were frequent visitors to the farm and their eyes lit up at the mention of the twin calves. They would have to go to the farm soon to see them.

After a special supper of roast chicken and crispy rashers, Gran turned to Lucy and said, 'So you'll be eleven on Sunday ... and aren't you growing tall? I've brought you a present but I won't give it to you until Sunday. That's your official present. But I've another for you — an unofficial one. My grandmother gave it to me just before my eleventh birthday ... and now I've giving it to you. There's only one condition! You have to hand it on to your daughter — or your grand-daughter — just before her eleventh birthday.'

She reached into her handbag and took out a small brown leather box which she handed to Lucy. Lucy opened it and her eyes opened wide. Inside was a beautiful ring. Set in a circle of white gold the dome-shaped stone was a rich deep red.

'It's a ruby ring,' said Gran. 'A star ruby. That means that

the stone has been cut in such a way that bands of light in the shape of a star appear in it. Take a closer look, Lucy.'

Jean McLaughlin was looking worried. 'You know, Gran, this seems much too valuable a gift to give to a child.' Her husband nodded.

Gran was adamant. 'Valuable or not, she has to have it. It was given to me just before my eleventh birthday — on condition that I passed it on to my daughter before her eleventh birthday. Well, as you know, I didn't have a daughter ... so it goes to Lucy. I can't break the trust.'

'But where did you get it?'

'Ah, that's a long story. And I'll tell it to you just as my grandmother told it to me.'

They all settled back. Gran had a great fund of stories, and Lucy and David loved listening to them.

'My grandmother would have been born about 1880. You can imagine what life was like in those days. Very hard! No chicken suppers or central heating or TV! Jobs were even harder to come by than they are today — if you can imagine that! There were very few openings for young boys of the poorer classes — and, believe me, at that time nearly everybody in Ireland was very very poor. They could stay on their tiny holdings and grow their few potatoes, or they could go into service at the local big house. They could emigrate to America or Australia ... or they could go into the British Army.

'Well, my grandmother's father had an uncle James who was rather wild. And nothing would do him but to join up. I think he thought he was going to fight in the Crimea but he didn't get there in time. The next thing he knew was that he was on board a ship heading for India. Did either of you hear of the Indian Mutiny?'

'No,' said David.

'The time the British were in India,' chanced Lucy.

Her grandmother's eyes twinkled. 'That covers a multitude! It was about the middle of the nineteenth century — I've forgotten the exact date. India was in turmoil, what between the Mohammedans and the Hindus, and anything could have sparked off a revolution. Just then the time was ripe. There was an old superstition that the British would only last in India for one hundred years, and it was just a century since Clive — you've heard of Clive, haven't you? — had come to India. Then the British issued a new kind of rifle and the rumour got round that the cartridges contained pig fat which was, of course, forbidden by the Hindu religion. There was a big uprising, and the British were besieged at a place called Lucknow. And guess where poor James ended up?'

'No!' said both children together.

'He was part of the small column of soldiers sent to relieve Lucknow. Which they did! And the British put down the Mutiny. But there had been many terrible atrocities, particularly the massacre at Cawnpore . . .'

'What was that?' interrupted Lucy.

'During the Mutiny, a certain Rajah called on the garrison at Cawnpore to surrender. He promised to spare their lives but as soon as they had given up their arms he had them all murdered, women, children and all, and thrown, dead and dying, into a well. So naturally tempers were inflamed and a terrible vengeance was exacted.'

'But what has all this got to do with the ring?' asked Lucy. Usually she loved to hear her grandmother telling stories but this time she wished she would get to the point.

'I'm coming to that. One night James was on sentry duty when he thought he saw a shadow moving in some rocks nearby. He rushed over and grabbed the man. It was an Indian, half-dead from injuries. He said he was a Rajah, that his palace had been sacked by the British and he had barely escaped with his life. At first, James was going to call his fellow soldiers but the poor Indian pleaded for his life. And he began to think to himself that it was rather odd for him, an Irishman, to be turning over a native Indian to the army of an invading nation. He may have been wild but he knew his country's history!

'So he hid the Rajah and a day later some followers of his came and took him away. Before he left, he said to James, "You have been very good to me. And I owe my life to you. Now I am going to give you something. It is very valuable — but you must never sell it. It has magic powers. It can grant wishes. Not to men. Only to women. I give it to you so that you can pass it on to your daughter or granddaughter."

'Now poor James was about to say he hadn't a daughter. Then he thought perhaps it might happen in the future. So he took the gift which the Rajah gave him — a small leather box...'

'This box,' breathed Lucy.

'The very one. When James opened it and saw the ring, he was naturally overwhelmed. Even *he* knew it was very valuable.

'Now, pass over a few years. James came back home to the old homestead and my grandmother's father — Thomas — welcomed him in. He had always had a soft spot for his uncle. However, he was married to a rather hard woman. Though they had only one child, my grandmother, the wife grudged every bite the old uncle took. But Thomas wouldn't hear of him being sent away.

'My grandmother became a great favourite with him. She nursed him whenever he got ill and they used to talk for hours together. He told her so many stories about the army and about India that I can't remember the half of them — you see, she told them all to me.

'When he got to the end of his days, just before he died, he called her in — everyone else had to leave the room — and gave her this little box, saying to her, "I want you to have this. I would have given it to your mother but she would only sell it — and this ring must never be sold. There is something magical about it, as I'm sure you will discover some day. I'm supposed to pass it on to my daughter but as I haven't got one, I think the Rajah would have approved of me giving it to you. Keep it, and when the time comes — how old are you by the way...?'

'I'll be eleven tomorrow,' said my grandmother proudly.

'Well, *you* can pass the ring on to your daughter or granddaughter before their eleventh birthday. It's a trust..."

'And this is the very same ring?' asked Lucy in awe.

'The very same. My grandmother had no daughters, so she kept the ring safely until I came along. And then, just before my eleventh birthday, she told me its story and gave it to me. And now, Lucy, I am passing it on to you...'

'I still think it's too valuable for a child,' said Paul. 'I'll put it in safe keeping for her.'

'Not until Monday,' begged Lucy. 'Just let me keep it till then.'

'All right,' agreed Jean. 'Gracious, look at the time. Off to bed with all of you. We've had enough excitement for one night. You, too, Gran. You must be exhausted.'

Before she got into bed, Lucy examined the ring again. It really was fantastic, she thought, as she slipped it on her left hand and turned it this way and that, admiring the deep rich glow of the ruby under the light. It was a bit loose for her but that didn't matter; she would soon grow into it. For a day that had started off badly, it had turned out wonderfully well. Now she only had to say her prayers — the short version tonight, she decided — and go to sleep. Tomorrow she would go and visit Noreen first thing and make up the quarrel...

She looked again at the ring, and it seemed to her that the ruby glowed with an extra intensity, drawing her eyes into the core of its brilliant red depths. Fascinated, she watched as the star shape within it seemed to flicker and grow.

As she was about to put it away, she accidentally knocked the little box off the table. It fell with a thud against the leg of the bedside table, and to her horror the lid split open. How, she thought in despair, would she ever tell Gran she had broken the box? When she picked it up, she found to her delight that it was not broken. The lid had simply split apart at a secret hinge. On the inside, in tiny gold lettering, some words were written, in writing so small that Lucy had to hold the box close to her bedside light to read it. The words made her heart race:

> *The secret of this Ruby Ring*
> *Is that two wishes it can bring,*
> *On right hand, middle finger, place*
> *Then turn the ring round but twice,*
> *Now make your wish, then wait and see,*
> *How magic the Ruby Ring can be.*

'Impossible!' thought Lucy to herself. 'And yet ...' What had the old soldier said? That there was something magical about it.

She read the words again. There was no mistake about the

message. The ruby ring was magic and it said she could have two wishes. Could this really be so? Had any other owner ever found the secret compartment? Had Gran? Did she make two wishes? Lucy determined to ask her the first time they were alone together.

In the meanwhile, she decided there was only one thing to do. She would have to test it for herself. But what would she wish for? 'I could wish for new clothes,' she mused. 'But what a silly waste ... I've plenty of clothes!' 'A pony?' She had always wanted a pony of her own. Should she? 'No!' she decided. If she got a pony her second wish would have to be for a stable. And ponies were quite expensive to keep. Her parents would probably insist she sell it. 'Her hair?' She liked her reddish-brown hair all right but she had often wondered what she would look like with blonde hair, maybe with a pink or green streak in it. With a giggle, she wondered what Mum and Dad and David would say if she came down to breakfast with such a hair style. But hair could be dyed; no use wasting a wish on that!

Then a little voice inside her seemed to say, 'What about a larger house, Lucy? You've always wanted to live in a large house.' That was true. She had wanted to live in a very large house ever since she could remember. Should she dare? 'Would it seem greedy?' she wondered. Still the message hadn't said anything about size.

She wondered if she should go downstairs first and ask Gran about it. But if Gran hadn't discovered the secret compartment and the tiny message, she might think a trial too dangerous and take the ring away.

'I'll test it myself first,' she decided, 'and if it works then I can surprise them all.' She wasn't quite sure how a larger house might materialise but she decided that if the ring was magic it could look after that detail.

She carefully read the words over yet again, and then she put the ring on the middle finger of her right hand. Turning it around twice, she closed her eyes and said, a little nervously, 'I wish to live in a much larger house than this.'

For some minutes nothing happened; just enough time for her to be glad she hadn't told Gran. Imagine believing that the twist of a ring could make a wish come true? She would have felt so silly.

But wait! Something peculiar *was* happening. She was wide-awake but her eyes would not stay open; no matter how she struggled she could not raise her drooping lids. Now something else ... she felt she was floating, and her tummy got that same churning feeling that she had had on The Octopus when the fun-fair came to town.

But soon these odd sensations ceased. The floating feeling did not last long, and now she was able to open her eyes again. 'Phew, thank goodness,' she thought. 'I got a fright there for a moment. I really thought something was happening.'

But her relief was short-lived. Her eyes, open now, widened in disbelief as she looked around her and her first bewildered thought was, 'I'm not in bed anymore; I'm outside. What is happening?'

A warm wind blew tendrils of hair about her face and the air was full of the sound of rustling trees. Looking down, she saw a roughly tied cloth bundle on the ground beside her. But before she had time to wonder too much what was in it, her horrified gaze fastened on the ugly black boots and thick black woollen stockings she was wearing. Her coarse brown dress fell well below her knees and a much patched brown cloak was tied around her shoulders. Putting up her hand to push away the hair from her eyes, she felt some sort of hat or bonnet on her head. Taking a deep breath, she took stock of her surroundings.

Facing her was a pair of tall wrought iron gates, set in two stately stone pillars which were surmounted by two massive stone globes. On either side the narrow road, fringed with whispering trees, stretched away until it was lost to view round a bend. 'What am I to do now?' she thought. For the first time she noticed the writing on the gate pillars. Carved deeply into the stone was the name Langley Castle. Peeping through the gates, she could see a small stone house to the left inside the gates. 'That can't be Langley Castle!' she concluded. 'It must be the gate lodge.'

Picking up her bundle, she pushed one of the heavy gates forward slightly and slipped through the opening. There was nobody in sight as she walked up the wide avenue lined with great trees, russet in their autumn colours. Beneath them grew banks of rhododendron bushes with glossy, dark-green leaves, shrubs with bright red berries whose names she did not know, and the occasional splash of the dark-red and purple of fuchsia bushes.

Around in a curve in the avenue, Langley Castle rose in all its glory, a graceful stone building, with mullioned windows, softly golden in tone, with shining pitched roofcaps of blue slate. On one side rose a square turreted keep and numerous chimneys were silhouetted against the skyline.

As she approached the house the trees and shrubs gradually gave way to wide green lawns. She crossed the sweep of gravel in front of the house and went up the stone steps leading to the front door. She had to stand on tiptoe to reach the heavy brass knocker.

Lifting it, she knocked once, and then again.

## 2  Langley Castle

Lucy jumped back when the massive door suddenly swung open. She stared mutely at the tall majestic man with the fringe of white hair, dressed in a peculiar-looking black coat that only reached his waist in front but descended half way down his legs at the back. His eyebrows were almost touching as he frowned down at her and said, 'Who are you, and what do you want?'

Lucy found to her amazement that she was incapable of speech. She opened her mouth but no sound emerged.

Looking at her more closely, the man continued, 'Ah, you must be the new maid. Round to the back, girl, to the servants' entrance,' he gestured with his left hand. 'And never use this door again. Do I make myself clear?'

Lucy flushed scarlet. She had never been spoken to like that in her life before. She was about to say, 'Yes, that's perfectly clear, thank you ... and I think that coat you're wearing looks awfully silly on you,' when the door was shut in her face.

She went down the steps and turned left to follow the driveway around the side of the house. Looking up as she walked, she saw more chimneys, each with four or five pots on top, and more and more windows. 'The place must be huge,' she thought. The ground sloped downward to a wide stone archway which led into a paved courtyard. To her right she saw a door with a black knocker and a black latch. Just as she was debating with herself whether she should knock or just walk straight in, the door was opened by a thin, freckle-faced girl in a dark dress and blue apron, whose black curls

were partially covered by a white cotton cap. With a friendly
smile she said, 'Hello, we weren't expecting you so early. I'm
just on my way to the gardens with a message but I'd better
take you in to Cook first. It's this way. I'm Nellie, the scullery-
maid. What's your name?'

'Lucy,' said Lucy as she followed Nellie along the stone-
floored passage which had a high coved ceiling. On either side
were doors marked 'Fish', 'Cooked Meat', 'Fresh Meat', 'Ice',
'Gun Room', 'Coal'. At the end of the long corridor, Nellie
took a right turn and opened a wide door with two glass panels
on top and they descended three stone steps into a huge kitchen.
The first thing that Lucy's confused mind took in was the
high ceiling and the tall iron girders supporting it. The window,
set high in one wall, had bars on the outside and she realised
that these were the smaller windows she had noticed on the
ground floor of the castle; 'Half the kitchen must be under-
ground,' she decided. Along one wall was a great wooden
dresser, laden with rows of copper saucepans, each numbered,

and ornamental moulds also of copper. Earthenware jars and colourful tin boxes stood on the dresser shelf and beneath it were drawers and doors.

A very fat woman was rolling out pastry at one end of the long table. One maid was chopping some turnips and onions, and another was cutting a loaf of bread.

'No one seems surprised to see me,' Lucy thought to herself. 'I wonder why not.'

She was about to find out.

Wiping her hands on the white apron that covered her long dark-blue dress, the fat woman said, 'So you're Brigid McIntyre's niece.' Lucy noticed that one cheek was smudged with flour which disappeared into a fold of flesh when she smiled.

'Her name's Lucy,' Nellie supplied helpfully.

'Will you run along to the gardens with that message and come back here sharp?' the cook said irritably. 'And you, Florrie, stop gaping and bring the wee girl a cup of buttermilk. She must be thirsty after her long walk. Now,' to Lucy, 'sit down there and I'll tell you the way things work here.' She turned the pastry a few more times and cut out some scone shapes with a fluted tin cutter. As she worked, her head bobbed up and down which made her stiff white collar dig into her double chin, and shook her small, white, frilled cap.

Lucy suppressed a smile and sat on the bare wooden chair.

'My name is Mrs O'Shea and I'm the cook. And a very fine cook I've heard it said. Down here in the kitchen, I'm the boss. Don't ever touch anything in this kitchen without asking my permission first and we'll get on all right. And always remember to use the back staircase. You're not to be seen on the main stairs without permission from your betters. And . . . now that I think of it . . . how is your aunt getting on?'

Lucy hesitated, thinking, 'Gosh, what am I going to say? Should I say that it's all a mistake?'

But the cook was chattering on. 'One of the best dairy-maids we've had at Langley. Pity about the accident. Scalding the churn she was and burned the whole arm. Still she'll be back in a few weeks and then you'll have a familiar face around the place. Now,' she continued importantly, 'Mrs Morris, the housekeeper, is not here at the moment but she left instructions that you are to work in the nursery wing mainly. You shouldn't find that too hard. What age are you, by the way?'

'Eleven,' Lucy answered.

'Eleven?' echoed Mrs O'Shea, and even Florrie who had just come back with a cup in her hand, stared in amazement. 'God between us and all harm. Why you'd make two of Nellie and she's fourteen. You must be mistaken. You're at least fifteen.'

Lucy thought it wiser not to argue. Instead she gulped down the buttermilk which, after the initial shock of unfamiliarity, she found pleasant and indeed refreshing.

Another maid came in and saying, 'Thanks, Mrs O'Shea,' took the tray of scones and put it into one side of the huge black range. Lucy had never seen a range like it before. It took up almost the whole wall and had numerous doors and knobs. A fire blazed behind the iron grating and above the range, set into the chimney breast, were two doors with glass fronts. Lucy could see plates sitting on the shelves behind the glass. 'So that's how they heat the plates,' she decided.

'If you're finished,' Mrs O'Shea's voice cut across her thoughts, 'Nellie will show you to your room, and then take you to the nursery wing. Hurry along now, there's work to be done. You mustn't imagine life is always like this,' she winked at Florrie. 'Come the end of the month there'll be no sitting around drinking buttermilk and eating scones. It'll be all scuddin' when the family gets back.'

Picking up her bundle, Lucy followed Nellie who opened a door beside the dresser, revealing a narrow flight of stairs.

'This is the servants' stairs,' she explained, 'the one we always use.' After climbing the first narrow flight they came to a green baize door studded with rows of brass discs. Lucy was about to open it when Nellie hissed, 'Not that way. That leads into the great hall. We keep going up the stairs.'

Lucy was intrigued. She would have liked to have seen what the great hall looked like. Maybe she would get a chance later. Nellie had already disappeared up another flight of stairs. A second baize door opened to the left but Nellie shook up her head. 'That leads to the nursery wing. We'll go there later. But our rooms are up another flight. Up we go again,' she grinned, taking the stairs two at a time while Lucy groaned and followed at a slower pace.

When she reached the top, Nellie led the way along a long gloomy corridor, the only light coming from the two small windows at either end. The bare floorboards creaked and groaned, seemingly in agony, as they moved along.

'This is it.' Nellie opened a door and ushered Lucy into a tiny dark bedroom which contained two small beds, a narrow wardrobe, a washstand with a chipped jug and basin, and a small rickety chest of drawers. Standing on the bare floorboards, Lucy stared around her in horror. Surely they didn't expect

her to sleep in this awful room! There was one small curtainless window which was closed tightly, so that the room had a stale and musty smell.

'You're sharing this room with me, Lucy,' said Nellie, 'and I'll be right glad of the company. It can get very lonely up here on your own at night. Not that there's that much time to be mooning about. By the time you get to bed you're so tired you fall asleep the moment your head hits the pillow ... We make our own beds every morning and we have to keep the room tidy. The housekeeper examines it twice a week and she gets real cross if thing aren't as neat as ninepins ... Now, if you want to hang up your cloak in the wardrobe, you can put your other things away later. You have the bottom drawer ... Oh, and you'll find your chamber-pot under the washstand there.'

Lucy eyed the large white delph pottery with disdain. 'No loos! What a dump!' she thought.

'Better hurry now, or cook will be yelling for me,' Nellie said.

Back down the first flight of steps they went and Nellie led Lucy through the green baize door and then through one painted white. It was like entering another world.

A tall window facing her, hung with pale-pink satin curtains, lighted the long corridor. It was carpeted in deep red and on some half-moon tables were china ornaments that, even to Lucy's inexperienced eye, looked both beautiful and costly. Near the window, on two elaborately carved stands stood pink and gold pot containers which contained luxuriant maidenhair ferns. Large oil paintings, mostly landscapes with a few hunting scenes, were hung on the pale cream walls.

Nellie halted outside a mahogany door and, knocking gently, entered, with Lucy at her heels. They were now in a large room where a fire blazed cheerfully in an open fireplace. The floorboards were stained almost black and a small carpet covered the centre of the room. A tall handsome woman with dark

eyes, wearing a green dress, her hair drawn back from her
pale face, was sitting at a table which was covered with a brown
fringed velvet cloth. A boy and girl sat reading aloud from
a book — it was *Treasure Island,* one of her own favourites
— but when they saw Lucy they stopped reading and stared
at her with open curiosity.

'That must be the governess, and they must be the children
of the house. But why did Mrs O'Shea say the family wouldn't
be back until the end of the month? Are there more?' Lucy
was puzzled.

'This is Lucy,' said Nellie. 'And she's only eleven, Miss
Wade.'

'Hello, Lucy,' said Miss Wade pleasantly. 'You seem a fine
strong girl for eleven, so I'm sure you'll be well able for the
work here. Now, Nellie, I'm sure Cook will be needing you,
so off you go and I'll show Lucy what to do.'

Robert stood up as Miss Wade said, 'This is Miss Elizabeth
and this is Master Robert.'

Robert, who looked about ten (though Lucy was by now
completely confused about age) gave her a friendly smile. Lucy
thought he looked very smart in his grey-and-green striped
blazer, though she wasn't very keen on the trousers, which
were buttoned just beneath the knees, or the long woollen
socks which were pulled up to meet the trousers. David would
be in hysterics about Robert's hair if he could see it; it was
parted in the middle and the straight blonde hair was combed
carefully to either side.

Elizabeth (would she be about twelve?) looked her up and
down and gave a yawn. Her long blonde hair was in ringlets,
held back by a large white ribbon. She was wearing a white
frilly pinafore over a blue plaid dress and she would have been
a very pretty picture indeed had it not been for the petulant
downward cast of her mouth. Lucy, aware of how shabby she
must look in her coarse brown stuff dress, could feel herself
disliking her right away.

Turning to Miss Wade, Elizabeth said snappily, 'I do hope she's better than the last one we had.' To Lucy she said, 'I want the schoolroom fire lit not later than seven o'clock each morning. It's bad enough not having fires in our rooms every morning but when there's none in the schoolroom it's intolerable.'

Glancing at her sharply, Miss Wade said, 'You're lucky to have a fire in the schoolroom at all. Many children don't. Just carry on with your reading, and, Lucy, you come along with me and I'll show you around.'

The children had a complete wing to themselves, the sitting-room that Lucy had just seen, a schoolroom and three bedrooms. The first, belonging to the governess, was large and partly furnished as a sitting-room, Robert's was spartan, with linoleum on the floor and dark furniture, while Elizabeth's had a carpet which was partly covered with a beige drugget; the curtains and bed coverlet were in a depressing brown print. On the window-sill were three dolls dressed in beautiful lacy dresses.

Lucy thought the children's rooms not half as colourful or comfortable as her own in Glenoran. But compared to her cramped miserable quarters upstairs at Langley, they were the height of luxury.

As Miss Wade moved from room to room she was explaining to Lucy just what her daily routine would be. With a start, Lucy realised that she had better concentrate.

'. . . Six o'clock sharp,' Miss Wade was saying. 'First thing is to open the shutters of the sitting-room and schoolroom. Take up the sitting-room rug, sweep both rooms, brushing the dust towards the fireplace. Lay your cloth in front of the fireplaces and put your box on it — I'll show you where everything is later. Rake out the ashes and put them in the cinder box. Then you black-lead the grates, and brush and polish every part.

'Now you lay the fire. Can you lay a fire, Lucy?'

'No,' said Lucy truthfully. At home Mum and Dad never allowed her to light the fire.

'Dear, dear,' Miss Wade smiled. 'I sometimes wonder what they teach you in those places. Well, I'll show you how. My fire wasn't cleaned out today so you'll have a perfect opportunity to see how it's done.

'When you've lit the fires, brush the rug in the sitting-room. Be sure you sprinkle it first with tea-leaves — they keep down the dust and give a pleasant fragrance. Your last job will be to dust the furniture — and don't forget the mantelpiece, shelves and the picture frames.' Lucy had noticed that the walls were hung with Victorian prints of children and dogs and horses — all very old-fashioned looking.

'Remember, Lucy, it's not enough just to flick a brush or a duster over the surfaces. Everything must be thoroughly rubbed so that there's not a speck of dust left. Oh, and don't forget the bookcase in the schoolroom. Every pane must be wiped and polished. Are you following all this?'

'Yes,' replied Lucy, feeling dazed.

'The children and I rise about seven o'clock, so the sitting-room and schoolroom must be in perfect order by then. Your next job will be to bring up hot water for the three of us — it should be there on the dot of seven. After washing and dressing, the children have various things to do — practising the piano and so on. You bring up the breakfast at eight, and after that ...'

'There's *more* to it,' thought Lucy in horror.

'... you can begin work on my room and those of the children, following the same routine. Open up the windows so that the rooms are thoroughly aired. Before you begin cleaning, take off all the bedclothes and put them over the backs of the chairs. Then empty the slops into the slop-bucket. And do make sure the ewers and basins are emptied and cleaned thoroughly. Finally, empty the water-jugs and wash and dry them before refilling. Then all you have to do is to remake the beds and leave the rooms neat and tidy.'

As she finished, Miss Wade said, 'I know this sounds quite a lot but you'll soon get used to the routine and you'll find you get through the work very quickly ... and at least you don't have to polish all the furniture every day — once a week will be enough.'

'How on earth am I going to remember all this?' thought Lucy in panic, but aloud she said, 'I'll do my best.'

'Sometimes,' continued Miss Wade, 'I eat with Mrs Morris, the housekeeper, in her room, but usually I have my meals in the schoolroom with the children. Can you tell the time, Lucy?'

'Oh yes,' said Lucy in surprise.

'It's "Yes, Miss Wade,"' said Miss Wade smiling. 'We have breakfast at eight o'clock, lunch at twelve-thirty, tea at four-thirty, and supper at seven o'clock. So remember those hours as I like to be punctual.' Returning to the schoolroom, she glanced at the clock on the mantelpiece and said, 'It's now a quarter past four, so that will just give you time to bring up our tea-trays. Off you go now, and remember to use the back stairs.'

Lucy went down the corridor, opened first the white door and then the baize door and rushed downstairs. The maid who had put the scones into the oven already had the children's tray ready.

'Is that all they are getting?' Lucy looked in amazement at the plate of bread and butter. Putting two glasses of milk on the tray, the maid said, 'Hurry back for Miss Wade's tray.'

Lucy found it quite hard work going up all those stairs, even though the tray was relatively light. When she got to the nursery wing, the hands of the clock showed twenty minutes to five.

Elizabeth, who had noticed the quick glance Lucy had given at the clock, said spitefully, 'Miss Wade, she's late and I've been longing for tea.'

'What a sly bag she is,' fumed Lucy.

Robert threw her a sympathetic glance and Miss Wade, frowning, turned to Elizabeth. 'Lucy is doing quite well for her first time. Now fetch my tray, child.'

Miss Wade's tray had a plate of hot scones and another with two thick slices of fruit-cake on it. 'That's more like it,' thought Lucy, suddenly realising how hungry she was; she hoped there would be fruit-cake for her tea too. She managed the stairs at a faster pace this time and was rewarded with a smile from the governess. 'We will be finished in about half an hour,' Miss Wade said, 'and you can collect the trays then.'

'Miss Wade seems a fair-minded person,' she reflected as she raced down the stairs. 'Robert is fine, but Elizabeth! What a pain!'

When she got back to the kitchen, there was nobody there. She was at a loss what to do when Florrie put her head around the door, saying, 'So you're back.'

'Yes, Miss Wade told me to have my tea down here, but there is nobody about.'

'Oh we don't take our meals in the kitchen, we eat in the servants' hall. Come along and I'll show you.'

Following Florrie through a door just beyond the big range, Lucy found herself in another stone-floored passage. Just below the ceiling was a long board to which bells were attached. Noticing her glance, Florrie explained, 'Each bell is for a different room. When one rings, someone has to dash up to that room immediately!'

They continued along the passage. 'There are just so many rooms and corridors,' Lucy said in exasperation.

Florrie laughed. 'Yes, it always takes the new girls ages to find their way around.' As they passed a door she nodded towards it. 'That's the housekeeper's room, just beside the still-room.'

'I don't think any of the rooms were moving,' Lucy said with a grin.

Florrie looked at her pityingly, then continued. 'It's where the housekeeper makes cordials and attends to pickling the vegetables and preserving the fruit... If we turned right up there we'd come to the butler's pantry and stores, but we're going in here — to the servants' hall.'

She led the way into a large room, much like the kitchen, with a floor of stone flags, but there was a cheerful open fire. A smaller dresser held plates and cups and saucers. The room seemed to be full of people, all sitting around the centre table.

Over the hub of voices, Florrie said, 'You can sit there beside Nellie.'

Lucy slid into a chair, conscious that all conversation had stopped and that the other servants were eyeing her curiously.

'I must be the only girl here without a white cap ... and I do wish I could get rid of this horrid brown dress.' Lucy was acutely conscious that she must look like an uncouth country cousin.

'This is Lucy, Brigid McIntyre's niece. She's going to work in the nursery,' explained Mrs O'Shea. The other servants smiled at her and a plump young woman at one end of the table poured out two cups of tea from the large brown glazed delph teapot beside her and they were passed along to Lucy and Nellie.

'That's Becky,' whispered Nellie. 'She's the head laundry-maid.'

Lucy was hungry. There was no fruit-cake on the table but there were plates of plain buns and gooseberry jam which satisfied her. As she finished her second bun, Nellie passed her another plate and said, 'Have a slice.'

'What is it?' Lucy eyed the yellow slices doubtfully.

'Haven't you had Indian corn bread before?' asked Nellie in surprise.

'Yes, of course,' said Lucy, not wanting to draw attention to herself, 'only we usually had it first.' She took a slice and spread some butter thinly on it. It tasted surprisingly good and she took another.

'Which one is the housekeeper?' whispered Lucy to Nellie in between mouthfuls.

'Oh, you won't see her, except at dinner. She has her breakfast, tea and supper in her own room, along with the butler, her ladyship's maid and the valet.'

'The butler?' asked Lucy. 'Is he nearly bald with just a little bit of white hair?'

'Yes, that's Winters all right. Very grand. Comes from London. But where did you meet him?' Then, with a gasp, 'Lucy, you surely didn't go to the front door, did you?'

Lucy reddened, then said defensively, 'Well, how was I to know?' Remembering her frosty reception she had to giggle, and she thought how well the name suited him.

When tea was over, the servants settled themselves on chairs near the fire, and some of them took out sewing or knitting. A man came in with a large tray and started to clear the tea things. With a guilty start, Lucy remembered the trays in the nursery and she went off.

The nursery teas were finished and Miss Wade had thoughtfully placed everything on the larger tray. She told Lucy to come back when she had brought the trays down as the fires had to be lit for the evening.

'What a life!' thought Lucy. 'Nothing but stairs.' Having left the trays in the kitchen, she raced upstairs again. Miss Wade opened a room off the sitting-room and said, 'This is where the sweeping brushes and dusters are kept. Here is your housemaid's box — black-lead, blacking and polishing brushes, emery-paper, cloth, leathers. Do remember that it is up to you to keep it well stocked. Now take it out, together with the cinder pail and the box with the wood and paper.'

In the governess's room, Miss Wade told her to roll back the small carpet, lay her cloth in front of the grate, and rake out the ashes into the cinder pail.

'Where are the firelighters?' asked Lucy.

In bewilderment, Miss Wade said, 'Firelighters?' Then with a laugh she said, 'Is that what you call them? Here you are,' and she handed Lucy the box which contained small pieces of wood and some paper twisted into coils. 'No firelighters,' groaned Lucy to herself. 'They're really out of the ark.'

Miss Wade was speaking again. 'Always put some cinders in the grate first.' Seeing Lucy's blank look, she said, 'Perhaps I should show you how we do it here, Lucy, and then you can carry on.'

'Thank you, Miss Wade,' said a relieved Lucy, following the governess into her room. There was a low brass fender in front of the fire and some lovely long-handled brass fire-irons.

'We don't use the good fire-irons everyday,' Miss Wade explained, as she showed Lucy the dull black tongs, poker and shovel which hung behind the polished wooden box that stood to one side of the fire.

Taking the lid off the cinder pail, Miss Wade removed some of the cinders. 'Now, Lucy, first we place some cinders in the grate, then some paper and we need about a dozen pieces of dry wood, or firelighters as you call them. Lastly, I'll place some pieces of coal on top of the wood, leaving space so that the air can circulate freely. Always remember to set your fire well back in the grate so that the smoke goes straight up the chimney and not into the room.' Reaching to the mantelpiece above, she took a box of matches and lit the fire. 'We'll soon have a nice fire ... now you can carry on and light the fires in Master Robert and Miss Elizabeth's rooms.'

Lucy, now feeling more confident, carried her box into Robert's room, set the fire as carefully as she could, and then went into Elizabeth's room. Catching sight of herself in the mirror that hung above the washstand — a tired-looking girl, auburn hair plaited and wound around her head — she thought how terrible she looked. She went back to the sitting-room, where one of the maids was lighting the oil lamps and drawing the curtains. Just then there was a cry from Elizabeth.

'Miss Wade, Miss Wade! I think the silly girl has put my room on fire. It's all smoke.'

Miss Wade and Lucy both rushed to Elizabeth's room. The room was full of smoke which was billowing from the fireplace.

'And look at the fire in Robert's room ...' Elizabeth had gone through to Robert's room, 'it's gone out!'

Miss Wade looked at both fires and spoke sternly to Lucy. 'I don't think you could have been listening to me properly when I told you how to set fires. Miss Elizabeth's was far too near the front of the grate — and there was no room for air in Master Robert's ... Ethel, would you show Lucy how we light fires in Langley?'

Cheeks scarlet at the reprimand, Lucy followed Ethel into Robert's room. She had seen Ethel at tea and thought she looked very pretty, with her long black dress, white frilly apron and the small white cap with two streamers down the back perched on her brown curls. With tongs, Ethel deftly reset the fire and lit it again. Then, in Elizabeth's room she moved the coals back and added more paper and sticks. She smiled at Lucy and said consolingly, 'Don't worry. You will soon get the hang of it.'

They looked into Robert's room and the fire was blazing brightly.

'Hurry, Lucy,' said Miss Wade as Lucy returned to the sitting-room. 'Run along for our supper trays. It's almost seven o'clock.'

Elizabeth gave her a triumphant glance from the corner where she was working, then exclaimed, 'Oh, look, Miss Wade. I've upset my work-box all over the floor. She'll have to clear it up.'

'When she's brought up the supper trays,' said Miss Wade wearily.

The oil lamps had been lit in the corridor and also at intervals down the stairs. In the kitchen Cook was busy slicing a ham when Lucy arrived in the kitchen, and Florrie was putting a plate of small biscuits on the tray beside the blue and white teapot. 'That's for Miss Wade.'

'Get the rice snowballs and custard for the children,' barked Mrs O'Shea. Lucy, who hated rice, watched with a shudder as Florrie tipped two balls of cold rice from small round bowls into a glass dish and poured custard over them.

As Lucy, on hands and knees in the corner, picked up the bits and pieces from Elizabeth's work-box, the children talked.

'It'll soon be time for Mamma and Papa to come home, won't it?' asked Elizabeth.

'Yes, they'll be back in a few days. And then we'll have all the preparations for the house party,' said Miss Wade.

'Well, I hope I'll be allowed down for dinner this time,' said Elizabeth. 'Papa promised me I could.'

'I don't know.' Miss Wade sounded dubious. 'You know Lady Tyrconnell said you would have to be fifteen before ...'

'It's so unfair,' burst out Elizabeth. 'Everyone treats me as if I were the same age as Robert. I'm two years older. I want to be treated as a grown-up, not a baby. I suppose it'll just be tea again this year. I'm so sick of it. Everyone saying, "Isn't Elizabeth getting tall?" "Isn't her hair a lovely colour?" "Aren't her cheeks pink?" I don't think I'll go to tea at all this year.'

'Elizabeth!' Miss Wade sounded shocked. 'You mustn't talk like that. If your mother says so, you must go down and meet her guests.'

Elizabeth muttered something under her breath and flounced from the room.

'I'm glad I don't have to look after her,' reflected Lucy as she tidied up the last of the spools and left the room, to the last injunction of Miss Wade, 'Now do remember — hot water at seven in the morning.'

When she closed the green baize door beyond the nursery corridor, Lucy leant against the wall, hot tears flooding her eyes. Why was she here in this terrible house, with everyone shouting at her, looking like the worst kind of skivvy, and nothing but work ... work ... work? It was all so unfair. When she had wished for a larger house she certainly hadn't expected anything like this. 'So much for ruby rings and their magic two wishes,' she felt savagely.

Suddenly she froze. Two wishes! What was the matter with her? The ring! How could she possibly have forgotten! She had one wish left. She could wish herself at home again. Just two twists and she would be safely back in Glenoran, with all the comforts of civilization, two loving parents, and David — Lucy remembered how excited he had been over the present he was going to give her on her birthday and how she had snapped at him because she was so upset over the essay competition. How long ago it all seemed now — and how trivial! 'I'll be much nicer to him in future,' she vowed.

Now she wondered how soon she should make her wish. It would have been nice to have seen the rest of the house and to learn more about life downstairs. And poor Nellie would be lonely again tonight on her own. Then she thought of all the work and the horrid Elizabeth and decided. She must get back to her own world — *tonight*. Besides, if her parents didn't find her in her room in the morning they would be so worried.

Her hands were shaking when she put down the tray on the stairs behind her and sat down, ready to make her second wish. As her gaze came to rest on her right hand she gave a gasp of horror. Her finger was bare! The ring was gone!

Gazing numbly at her hand, Lucy wondered where on earth the ring could be. There was a pocket in the ugly brown dress and, trying to still her trembling hands, she searched frantically. Still no ring. Her thoughts were in a whirl at first. Then she forced herself to try and think clearly. Maybe the ring was in the bundle in her room. Maybe there was a pocket in the cloak and the ring had somehow slipped off her finger — it was loose after all — and was in that pocket. That must be it! No need to panic! 'Magic is very strange,' she thought. It made her forget all about the ring for a while. But now that she had remembered, all that she had to do was to find it and wish!

Wiping away the tears that had trickled down her cheeks, she raced up the stairs to the bedroom. Her heart was thumping with excitement as she turned the wooden knob of the door, but before she could enter, a voice sounded behind her.

'You there, girl, stop immediately!' Lucy froze into stillness as a tall thin woman came along the corridor towards her, the large bunch of keys hung from her waist jangling noisily as she moved. 'Are you the new girl for the nursery?'

'Yes, I'm Lucy,' was the nervous reply, her hand still on the knob of the door.

'I am Mrs Morris, the housekeeper, and I am in charge of running this house. Your aunt Brigid spoke to me about this situation for you. She said you were a sensible, reliable child. I hope she's right. But you are never to come to your room again when you are on duty. I'll make allowances for you this time as it's your first day, but don't let it happen again. Now get back to work. I was looking for you, as a

matter of fact. I want to give you your uniform. Come with me.'

'Yes, Mrs Morris,' said Lucy weakly, following the housekeeper down the stairs, picking up the tray on the way. 'What an old battle-axe. Still, I'll get back to my room at bedtime and then — good-bye to Langley for ever!'

In the housekeeper's room, Mrs Morris took some clothes from one of the presses lining the wall and handed them to Lucy. 'You have a blue print dress and a black one. The blue one is for the morning, the black one for the afternoon. When you're working at cleaning and laying the fires, you wear this dark-blue apron. In the afternoon, you wear the white apron. The big cap is for the morning and the frilly one for the afternoon.'

'Can I change now?' asked Lucy, thinking that she would get to her room again.

'No, don't bother for tonight. You are already late for supper, so run along to the servants' hall.'

There was no escape. Under the eagle eye of the housekeeper Lucy had to go down the corridor towards the servants' hall. A large oil lamp like the one in the kitchen was suspended above the long table, and most of the other servants were already at their supper. Somebody placed a plate before her 'Mutton pie,' whispered Nellie. It was good and, in spite of her worries, Lucy ate with relish. Along the table were plates piled high with bread and dishes of yellow butter.

At the head of the table, Mrs O'Shea was in high good humour. 'That's as may be,' she was saying to Florrie as Lucy came in. 'But what I say is that money does count. Look at this place. Going to rack and ruin before her Ladyship took over.'

'The Tyrconnells are one of the oldest families in Ireland,' said Florrie. 'Maybe they didn't have money but they had everything that counts. Breeding. A title going back to God goes when. What did the Langleys have but money?'

'Rack and ruin,' repeated Mrs O'Shea. 'Antiquity, yes — I'll grant you that. But *you* know what the house was like when her Ladyship came here first.'

'Nothing but a crumbling ruin,' sniffed Ethel.

'It was good enough for generations of the Lords of Tyrconnell.' Florrie was sounding heated.

'But not good enough for her Ladyship! Or for me for that matter.' Mrs O'Shea shook with laughter. 'I took one look at the place and says I to myself, "Is this was I left the comforts of Oxfordshire for? The cold ... the damp ... the leaking roof ... the mildewed walls?" I was on the point of giving my notice — and I know Winters and Ethel were too — when it turned out her Ladyship had great plans for the place. "Pull it down," she says, "and we'll build something decent." And so she did. Four years it took, but wasn't it worth it?'

'She got a title, didn't she? Florrie was even more heated. 'Wasn't that enough for her?' One that went back to the days of Red Hugh. And changing the name to Langley ...'

'Well, his Lordship has got a sound dry house, hasn't he? And bathrooms. I haven't heard *him* complaining about the comforts of Langley,' put in Ethel. 'And why wouldn't she change the name? It was her family money that built it.'

'To be fair, she didn't pull it *all* down. Only the front part. Isn't there plenty of the old castle still round at the back? And more's the pity to my mind. I'd have knocked the whole pile down.' Then seeing that Florrie was maintaining a cold silence, Mrs O'Shea continued, 'Now, don't take on so, Florrie. You know I wouldn't say a word against Lord Tyrconnell — the most upright gentleman that ever lived — a good landlord to his tenants, like all his family before him. I should know.'

She poured herself another cup of tea and looking down the table to Nellie, she said, 'You there, young Nellie. Did you know that I started my life here over forty years ago? As scullery-maid, just like you. Those were the real bad times, but the old Lord set up soup kitchens here in the castle. In

they came, lines and lines of them every day, so thin and so hungry. Some of them with barely a stitch on them. It was a terrible sight. 1846 that was.

'But, Florrie,' turning back to the kitchen-maid, 'if you'd worked here in those days, you wouldn't be complaining about what her Ladyship has done. I remember this kitchen ... and the cold of it. There would icicles hanging off the walls in the depth of winter. A body just couldn't get warm. Talk about ice! We could have picked it off the eaves then. Only we never heard of iced puddings in those days! Comfort is comfort, I say, and if money buys it, I'm all for money.'

'Some people are not too particular how they make their money,' said Florrie.

'Oh hers is respectable. Herrings and hemp to the Russians. Made her father a millionaire, in the days when a million was a million.' A sudden thought occurred to her and she laughed again. 'Did I ever tell you about the motto of the Langleys? They put the poor old herring on the coat of arms when he was made a baronet and the motto he chose was, *All good things come from above.* Very funny really, when you think his fortune came from below.'

'Why did you leave here?' asked Lucy. The seniors looked at her in amazement and she suddenly realised that neither she nor Nellie were expected to contribute to the conversation.

'A man, young Lucy, the cause of all the trouble in the world. I married Finty O'Shea. He was footman to the Duke of Netherton so he got me a job in the kitchens there. And up I rose until I became head cook. Then the Langleys offered me more, so I joined them. And when Louisa Langley married Lord Tyrconnell, I came back here with her. Always had a soft spot for this place — it was like coming home.'

'Miss Elizabeth takes after her Ladyship — and that's for sure,' said Florrie.

'And poor Master Robert takes after his father. If he has his way there won't be a penny left. Poor lad. No sense. Do you know what he said to me once, "Do you think we should own all this?" '

'What did you say to that?' asked Becky.

'I said to him, "If *you* don't own it, somebody will!" ... Well enough of that. We'd better start preparing for next week's shindig tomorrow. They'll be upon us before we know where we are. Florrie, we'll get the menus sorted out tomorrow. Mrs. Morris wants to see them. And we must check what's available. Nellie, run down to McDyer in the morning and see what vegetables and fruit he has. Well, at least, we'll have plenty of game. Are the Gordons coming this year?'

Ethel replied that they were which seemed to satisfy Mrs O'Shea. 'A great shot. I wouldn't say no to a nice plump woodcock right now. And Sweeney thinks there may be a few grouse about. It'll be mainly venison, I suspect. Perhaps a little widgeon. Nellie, get me out my game recipe book. His Lordship particularly commented on my *Salamis de Perdrix* last year. Said Lord Spencer was very taken with it. Pity we won't have the new Lord-Lieutenant this year. But I suppose he's too busy with Mister Parnell and the election . . .'

Lucy, whose attention had begun to waver and was now feverishly wondering if she would ever get upstairs to her room, gave a couple of noisy yawns. Mrs O'Shea looked down towards her.

'Time you were both off to bed. It's way past your bedtime. Nellie, Lucy, take your candles and off. You have to be up at five-thirty, remember.'

'If one more person tells me to remember something, I'll scream, 'muttered Lucy to herself as she took her candle and said good-night.

She could not race up the stairs for fear her candle might blow out, but she went as quickly as she could, much to the surprise of Nellie who trailed after her, up the gloomy staircase and along the corridor to her room, hardly noticing the creaking of the floorboards and the jumping shadows cast by the candle-light, which would have sent shivers up and down her spine in normal times.

In her room at last, she put the candle down on the chest

of drawers and pulled the long brown cloak from the wardrobe. Carefully she examined it. There *must* be a pocket; there just had to be a pocket. She went over it inch by inch, spreading it carefully out on the bed to make sure she had overlooked no tiny slit or crevice. But there was nothing.

With a sob of panic, she took out the bundle and tore it open, spreading the contents out on the bed. There was another hideous brown dress, two long loose slips, another garment that looked like a vest but had long sleeves and a high round neck, and two pairs of knickers gathered at the knees, just like the ones she was wearing. Apart from a face flannel, a comb and another pair of long black woollen stockings, that was all.

Taking the brown dress in her hands, Lucy found that it too had a pocket, but her frantic search yielded nothing. She carefully checked each item in the bundle. Again nothing. Eventually she gave up the search. Now she had to face the hard, terrifying truth. The ruby ring was gone. Where, she did not know. But one thing was clear. Until she found it, she was trapped in Langley Castle.

## 3  Elizabeth Makes a Discovery

During Lucy's frantic search, Nellie, who was by now in bed, had been watching her curiously.

'What on earth are you doing?' she asked at last.

'Just something I was looking for,' said Lucy dully. 'I'll have another look in the morning.'

A sudden surge of hope ran through her. Maybe the ring had dropped out of one of the garments, on to the floor. She would have to look, first thing in the morning.

'Better go to bed,' said Nellie. 'Otherwise you'll never be able to get up in the morning.'

With a heavy heart, Lucy replaced the cloak in the wardrobe, and hung the brown dress beside it. The other things she folded and put in the empty second drawer of the chest. Then with fumbling fingers she undid the buttons of her dress and hung it beside the other one. Next she removed the long heavy slip. The black boots had been pinching her feet but it took her some time to undo the buttons at the sides and relieve her aching feet. She unfastened the button at the side of her knickers and threw them aside. Then she took off the long black stockings; these had been held up by elastic bands which had left ugly red marks on her thighs. At last she was down to the long-sleeved vest which scratched her skin, but she decided to leave it on as the room was quite chilly and quickly pulled on one of the stiff nightdresses over it.

'What a longsome procedure,' she sighed as she climbed into bed and tried to make herself comfortable on the lumpy mattress. The tears which she had so bravely held back were building up behind her closed eyelids and finally she could restrain them no more.

Nellie, hearing her sobs, was quick to comfort her. 'Don't fret, Lucy, it will take you a wee while to settle in and then you'll love it.'

'But I don't belong here, Nellie,' sobbed Lucy.

'I felt like that too when I came first, but now that I've got to know the other girls it's different.'

Lucy was about to explain about the ring. Then she realised that Nellie would never understand that she came from another age so she said nothing.

'They feed you well here,' Nellie said encouragingly. 'Mind you it's not the same as they get in the housekeeper's room. That's really grand.' She began to giggle. 'Mrs O'Shea told us once about some lord in England. He was always complaining about the food and one day he called the butler and said to him, "I don't expect to have as good food as you have in the housekeeper's room, but I must insist on its being the same as in the servants' hall."'

Seeing Lucy smile for the first time, Nellie went on, 'It's true! I haven't been hungry for a day since I came here.'

Forgetting her own troubles, Lucy sat up and asked, 'Were you often hungry then, before you came here?'

'Oh, aye, often. I'll never forget that sick, empty feeling in the pit of me stomach. But that was when I was on me own. It was a bad time. Best to forget it.'

'Are your family dead?' asked Lucy sympathetically.

'No, not dead, but as good as,' Nellie said flatly, adding in a whisper, 'They're in America. All of them, except me of course ...'

Immediately Lucy thought of several questions she would have liked to ask Nellie, but the scullery-maid's face had taken on a sad closed look that made her hesitate to intrude. Instead she said, 'There must be a very large family living here as there are so many servants.'

Nellie smiled and said, 'There's just Miss Elizabeth and

Master Robert. And of course Lord and Lady Tyrconnell — only they're not here half the time. They usually go to the South of France in the spring, then here, then the Season in London, then back here, then the grouse shooting in Scotland, then to Langley again for more shooting. And of course Spencer and Fox are with them.'

'Who on earth are Spencer and Fox?' asked Lucy.

'Her Ladyship's maid and Lord Tyrconnell's valet. They always travel with them.'

'How strange to have all those servants to look after so few people,' Lucy said in astonishment.

'That's the way the gentry do it, Lucy. Anyway the place is enormous. You should hear Ethel and Minnie complaining about all the dusting and sweeping and clearing out grates and making beds that they have to do. Especially when there are people staying.'

'I met Ethel. Who's Minnie?'

'Minnie — she's away the day — is the under-housemaid, so she has to do most of the hard work. Ethel gets all the nice jobs like dusting the ornaments and polishing the furniture. Poor Minnie is down on her hands and knees most of the time, scrubbing and washing the floors. Ethel makes sure that Minnie does things right and then Mrs Morris comes along to make sure Ethel is doing things right too!'

'They must be kept very busy,' said Lucy thinking of the front of the house and of all the rooms that must lie behind all those windows.

'Not as bad as working in the kitchen,' said Nellie with feeling.

'Florrie is the kitchen-maid, isn't she?'

'Yes, and so is Maggie — you saw her when you arrived. They have to do all the scrubbing and sweeping in the kitchen, the servants' hall and the passages. And the front steps. All the heavy work is in the kitchen. And of course Florrie and Maggie have to help with the cooking too. They prepare the vegetables and the meat for Mrs O'Shea, and the meals for the servants' hall and the nursery and The Room.'

'The room?' asked Lucy curiously.

'The housekeeper's room. That's what we always call it ... Florrie also does the sauces and gravies.'

'Florrie is always arguing, isn't she?' asked Lucy.

'All the time. Especially with Ethel! Florrie and Maggie are sisters, you know.'

'They do look a bit alike,' said Lucy, thinking of the two broad faces and the red cheeks.

'Then there's Bella Jane. She's the still-room maid. She prepares the breakfast and the teas. Bakes the bread and scones and so on ...'

'She's the maid who put the scones in the oven, is she?'

'That's her. She was helping Mrs Morris today to make jams so Mrs O'Shea did the scones for her ... that's why she was thanking her. Though sometimes they have terrible rows ... you see the meat dishes for breakfast come from the kitchen and the rolls from Bella Jane and they have all sorts of arguments if things aren't ready together.'

'It's as bad as the unions,' thought Lucy. 'Talk about demarcation!' Aloud she said, 'And what do you do?'

'Everything that nobody else wants to do!' Nellie had recovered her good spirits. 'Principally all the dirty pots and pans and bowls, and I have to keep the scullery clean and help to prepare the vegetables — all the nasty bits.'

A sudden banging on the wall interrupted them.

'That's Florrie,' whispered Nellie. 'And indeed when I think of all that's ahead of me tomorrow, with this house party coming, I'd better get to sleep straightway.'

Nellie must have fallen asleep almost immediately because shortly afterwards Lucy heard her gentle regular breathing.

Lucy lay on her lumpy mattress, wide-eyed in the dark, and thought, 'What a strange day this has been!' Somehow her own troubles did not seem so bad now since hearing about

Nellie's life. Working in the scullery, washing pots and pans day in and day out, must be an awful life. Yet Nellie said it was better than going hungry. But how could her family have gone to America and left her behind? It seemed so cruel. Maybe Nellie would tell her more about it tomorrow night — if she was still here tomorrow night . . .

The thought of tomorrow brought her back to her own problems, and the missing ring. It must have dropped out of her dress or her cloak and was now lying on the floor. She would search first thing in the morning. If it was not in the room, maybe she lost it coming up the avenue. She was inclined to rule out the kitchen, the stairs and nursery. They were swept and brushed so often that it would surely have turned up by now. No, if it wasn't on the floor she must look on the avenue as soon as she got the opportunity. She blessed herself and said her prayers — the long version tonight — and after much tossing and turning she fell into a troubled sleep, her last conscious thought being of the clock on the chest of drawers that seemed to get louder and louder and louder . . .

She was awoken by someone shaking her roughly by the shoulder. Reluctantly opening her eyes, she saw Nellie in the dim candlelight, already dressed, urging her to get up quickly as it was almost six o'clock. 'Hurry,' she urged. 'You've got to light the nursery fire on time or that little monster Elizabeth will make trouble for you.'

With a groan, Lucy jumped out of bed. The bare floorboards chilled her feet and the cold water which she splashed on her face made her shudder. But it succeeded in jolting her into wakefulness. By now, Nellie was combing her dark curls and putting on her cap. Lucy was slow in getting dressed. Tears of frustration welled up in her eyes as she battled with the rows of small buttons down the front of the blue print dress. Seeing her difficulties, Nellie offered to comb and replait her hair for her, an offer Lucy accepted gratefully.

When Nellie went off down to the kitchen, Lucy lit her candle and on hands and knees searched the floor thoroughly. No ring! So she *must* have lost it on the avenue. Refusing to allow herself to panic, she quickly put on her blue apron and the white cap before pulling on the black woollen stockings and the wretched buttoned boots. Ready at last, she took her candle and trudged off to the nursery. The bracket oil lamps along the corridor were still dark but when she got to the nursery the lamp on the table had been lit.

Already late, she opened the shutters and hurriedly fetched her work-box and cinder pail, swept the floor, pulled back the carpet, put down her cloth and cleared out the dead cinders. She laid the fire, taking care to set it well back in the grate this time, as she had been shown. Then taking a bowl of tea-leaves from the brush room she sprinkled them on the carpet, then swept towards the fireplace. Now there was only the dusting to do. After that she tackled the schoolroom.

It all took time and Lucy was breathless when she had finished. Adding more coal to the fire that was starting to blaze up nicely, she was startled when the door opened and a tall dark-haired man, dressed in a dark jacket, waistcoat and trousers came in.

'Who are you?' she asked.

'McGinley, at your service,' giving a low bow. 'I'm the footman and you're Lucy, I'm told.'

'Yes,' Lucy had an answering smile, liking him right away.

'Well, don't mind me, young Lucy. I've only come for the lamps.' Seeing her look of surprise, he explained, 'It's part of my job to take the lamps down to the lamp room, clean the wicks, and refill them with oil. Then, abracadabra, they're ready for another night.'

'Oh, I see,' Lucy said, thinking to herself, 'There really is so much work running a house this size.'

When McGinley had gone Lucy went back to the window.

It was now light enough to see outside. The window looked down on the courtyard at the back of the house. Through a stone archway set in the back wall, she could glimpse another group of buildings. 'They must be the stables,' she told herself, wondering if she would ever find out for sure. Off to her right, she could see over the high stone wall that she had seen yesterday on her way to the servants' door and she could see flowers, trees and shrubs. 'How lovely, a walled garden ... goodness,' looking at the clock. 'I'd better hurry.'

When she brought back the jugs of hot water, Elizabeth was still asleep, looking like an angel with her blonde hair and pink and white complexion. 'Pity she doesn't sleep more often,' thought Lucy, tip-toeing to avoid waking her. Robert was already awake and gave her a cheerful smile.

A light was coming from under Miss Wade's door and when Lucy went in she was sitting at the dressing-table, still in her wrapper — a beautiful one of pale-blue silk with flowers embroidered on it — plaiting her long brown hair.

Lucy thought she looked most attractive and wondered why she had never married.

'Please pull back the curtain, Lucy,' said Miss Wade, 'and let us see what sort of a morning it is.' As the early morning sunlight flooded the room, Lucy's gaze came to rest on a silver-framed picture of a handsome man in uniform. Seeing her curious gaze, Miss Wade smiled sadly and said, 'He was my fiancée. He served with the British army. He was killed at the battle of Tel-el-Kebir.' Seeing Lucy's blank look, she said, 'That's in Egypt. He was serving in the Black Watch regiment. We were to be married the following spring. That's three years ago now — 1882 — and I still miss him dreadfully. But,' she added with a sigh, 'it does not do to dwell on the past. Life goes on and we must trust in God to heal the wound.' Looking at the clock, she said, 'You can do the fire after breakfast. Now, off you go.'

At last Lucy was free to eat her own breakfast and when a plate of porridge was placed before her, even though she hated porridge, she poured some creamy milk from the large blue and white jug over it and ate it with relish. Then she tackled thick slices of brown bread and butter.

Bella Jane greeted Lucy with a smile when she went to the kitchen. 'I've just put the porridge on the tray, wait until I get the eggs and toast. I'll have Miss Wade's tray ready by the time you get back.'

In the nursery, Elizabeth and Robert were seated at the table, which had been covered with a white cloth. As usual, Robert greeted her with a smile; Elizabeth said shortly, 'Do hurry up, I'm hungry.'

'And very rude too,' said Lucy to herself as she silently set the tray down and went off for Miss Wade's.

Maggie was getting covers for the small silver dishes on the governess's tray when Lucy came back into the kitchen. She was astonished to see that they contained kidneys, bacon and poached eggs.

'She'll never eat all that,' protested Lucy.

'No, I don't expect she will, but that's the way it's done here. There's even more choice than that in The Room — I've just sent their breakfast in — and you should see the dining-room when Lord and Lady Tyrconnell are here. The whole top of the sideboard is covered with dishes of bacon, eggs, kedgeree, kidneys, cutlets, kippers. They take a big breakfast — to keep them alive until luncheon! Then Winters and McGinley take out huge hampers of food, drink, tablecloths, cutlery and glasses ... Now,' as Bella Jane added rolls, 'here you are,' thrusting the tray into her hands.

When Lucy had carried down the nursery breakfast trays, she began on the three bedrooms: Sweeping, black-leading the fireplaces, setting the fires, dusting the furniture. The beds had to have every scrap of clothing taken off, the bed linen shaken out and then the beds made up again. By the time she got to Robert's room she was tired and stopped to rest for a minute.

The door to the schoolroom was open and she could hear the progress of the lessons inside. It was French and arithmetic this morning. Elizabeth answered everything, sharply and promptly. Robert was slower and Elizabeth often answered for him, sometimes translating the answer into French.

'Elizabeth,' said Miss Wade quietly. 'Do let Robert answer for himself. You're rushing him.'

'But he's so slow! And so stupid. I could do all those sums at his age, in half the time.'

'Elizabeth,' Miss Wade sounded weary and Lucy guessed that lessons were constantly punctuated by these exchanges. 'Robert may be slower than you were at his age, but he'll never learn if you keep interrupting. Now, Robert, don't mind her. Just write this down and take your time over the answer: If four men cut a meadow in one day, how long would it take two men to cut a meadow two and a half times bigger?'

'Does anything ever change?' Lucy chuckled to herself as

she tidied up the brush room. But hearing the lessons made her think of Noreen. How she wished she were back at her own school. And how she missed Noreen. 'When I get back I'll be a much better friend.' A disturbing image crossed her mind, of someone who was always interrupting to show that she knew the answers, and she blushed guiltily.

When she went back into the schoolroom, Elizabeth had a sketching-pad before her, and Miss Wade was sharpening some pencils.

'I've sketched everything in the room,' she was complaining.

'Why not sketch Lucy? She'll be a new subject for you.'

Elizabeth gave Lucy a contemptuous look, then said in a bored voice, 'Sit over there . . . where the light falls on you.'

' "Sit over there, *please*," ' Miss Wade corrected.

'Please, Lucy,' yawned Elizabeth.

'Always be polite to inferiors,' thought Lucy. 'It'll make you feel better — when you're kicking them around.'

Being a model was tiresome work. Every time she moved,

Elizabeth said sharply, 'Keep still. How can I sketch you if you keep changing your position?'

So the morning passed.

When Miss Wade called a halt to lessons, she let Lucy see the sketch. Lucy was surprised at how good it was. Compared to her own feeble efforts in drawing-class at school, this was more like the work of a grown-up. It was a true likeness — the slightly rebellious tilt of the head, the candid look in the eyes, the wayward hair escaping from under the cap, all faithfully captured.

'I'll finish it tomorrow,' said Elizabeth, throwing it aside.

As the children put away their slates and books in the large cupboard that stood against one wall, Miss Wade said, 'Come, I think we need some fresh air before lunch. We'll go to the stables and see how Darkie's lame leg is progressing — hopefully he will be better and you can go riding again next week. Then we'll have a walk in the garden and get some flowers for the schoolroom. Lucy, you may come too and carry the basket for the flowers. Go and get your cloak and you may walk down the main stairs with us. Elizabeth, I think you should wear your blue coat today.'

Lucy held her breath, excitement sweeping over her. Here at last was the chance she had been waiting for. She ran as fast as her long dress would allow her, got her cloak from the bedroom and quickly rejoined the others. Taking the basket the governess handed her, she followed them down the corridor until they came to a door.

Going through the door, she found herself on a very wide landing, lined with huge paintings of landscapes. Two curved staircases, one to the right and one of the left, swept down to the next landing, which had an open fireplace set into the wall. From the fireplace landing, a wide staircase descended to the ground floor. Lucy went down slowly, overawed by such grandeur. The hall was enormous, with tall marble columns rising to the high ceiling. Walking along the polished marble floor she could see into a room on her right with a shining parquet floor and chairs and sofas along the walls. Lucy wondered if that was the drawing-room. On her left, through another open door, she could see shelves running from floor to ceiling, all filled with books. That had to be the library. Ahead of her was the main entrance, and hurrying now, after the others, she went down the broad stone steps that she had used on her arrival. As they walked along the wide gravelled driveway, she kept her eyes down, eagerly scanning the ground. But there was no ring to be seen. As they turned through the stone archway to the back of the house, her hopes were dashed again. There was no flash of ruby light anywhere.

Miss Wade, calling on her not to lag behind, led the way through a second stone archway and Lucy found herself in a cobbled yard, with buildings around the four sides. In the centre block facing them, which had a weathercock flying from the roof, stone steps led to a door upstairs, but Miss Wade entered through the door on the ground floor and called, 'Are you there, Fielding?'

'Here in the tack-room, Miss,' came a voice and Lucy followed the others into a room where the walls were hung with bridles, reins, saddles and other items of harness, all neatly hung on wooden pegs. A small fire burned in the open grate and Fielding was sitting beside it polishing a small saddle.

'We've come to see how Darkie is getting along,' said Miss Wade.

'Doing fine, Miss. He'll be able for a little light work from tomorrow.'

'Well, hardly tomorrow — Sunday. But the children can start their riding again on Monday.'

As they were talking, Fielding led them down a wide passage which led to a stable with four stalls. In one of them stood a jet-black pony.

'Darkie,' squealed Robert, rushing forward and reaching up to stroke his nose. He opened the half-door and went in. Having examined the pony, he exclaimed, 'His leg seems better, Fielding.'

'Aye, that linament of Shaw's seems to have done the trick.'

'I must look at Sparkle,' said Elizabeth, going into the next stall where a chestnut pony with a white blaze on his forehead was stabled. 'Poor Sparkle, only getting dreary exercise with the boy. Never mind,' she held out her hand and the pony eagerly ate the apples she had, 'I'll be back on Monday and we'll have exciting gallops together.'

Lucy looked at her in amazement. This was a different Elizabeth from the spoilt supercilious girl of the nursery. Even her voice had changed, becoming warm and friendly.

They made their way back into the autumn sunshine, back through the kitchen courtyard and along a gravelled path that had a high wall on one side and a sweep of lawn on the other. When they came to a green painted door set neatly into the gray stone wall, Miss Wade lifted the latch and they stepped into the walled garden. Lucy sighed with delight at the riot of colour. Clumps of ox-eye daisies, lilac-coloured michaelmas daisies, asters in glowing red and snowy-white, grew in borders with tall yellow and pink gladioli and banks of dahlias in all the colours of the rainbow. As they moved along the paved pathways, Miss Wade stopped every now and again to cut some flowers. When she had added yellow and red snapdragons to the dahlias and daisies she had picked, she decided they had enough and should go back to the house.

Lucy's mind was racing. She just had to get down the avenue to look for her ring — it *must* be there. She now felt sure that she would have noticed if it had fallen off in the house. So it must be somewhere along the avenue. That is, if nobody had already found it. She shivered at the thought.

Passing the sweetly scented roses that grew against the wall beside the green door, Miss Wade and Robert were ahead of her, with Elizabeth following behind. This suited her hastily formed plan, so with fingers crossed and taking a deep breath she suddenly started to limp. Then she stopped and putting her basket down she started to rub her ankle.

Seeing this, Elizabeth called, 'Come, Lucy, surely a short walk isn't too much for you.'

'Oh, Miss Elizabeth, it's these boots. One is rubbing my ankle and it's quite sore. I'm glad we don't have to walk down the avenue as well.'

'Indeed! Well, I'd like a walk down the avenue, so you'll have to come too. You're only a servant and will do as you are told.'

'Yes, Miss Elizabeth,' said Lucy meekly, keeping her head down to hide her smile. It looked as if her plan might work!

Skipping ahead now, Elizabeth called to the governess, 'Miss Wade, let's go down to the gatehouse and look at Tara's new puppies.'

'Yes, let's,' said Robert enthusiastically. 'Fielding says we can give them names.'

'Very well,' said Miss Wade looking at her watch. 'We'll just have time before luncheon. I've been looking forward to seeing Tara's puppies myself.'

They set off at a fast pace down the avenue, Lucy with head bent, eyes vainly searching for her ring.

When they reached the gatehouse, the governess knocked and waited. The door was opened by a grey-haired man in a striped shirt and waistcoat.

'Good morning, Jim. We've come to take a look at Tara's puppies,' said Miss Wade pleasantly.

'Certainly, come this way,' and Jim led the way around the side of the house. 'Now Miss Elizabeth and Master Robert, here they are?' He opened the outhouse door, and there in a basket were five tiny pups. Their mother, a beautiful red setter, stood protectively beside them.

'Oh, Jim, they're beautiful,' said the children together. 'We must give them nice names.'

'Nothing too fancy now,' said Jim. 'His Lordship will want

them as gun-dogs, so he'll want sensible names.'

'I think we should call this little fellow Rusty,' said Robert.

Elizabeth agreed and they quickly named three more, Bruno, Brandy and Jessie. Then inspiration ran out.

'What about Red Hugh?' suggested Miss Wade.

'Yes.' Elizabeth picked up the biggest and strongest of the litter. 'That's just right — he's the chieftain.'

They said good-bye to Jim and the puppies and set off up the avenue again. Elizabeth ran ahead of the others, reciting, 'Rusty, Bruno, Brandy, Jessie, Red Hugh.'

Suddenly she stopped and called excitedly, 'Miss Wade, do come quickly.'

The governess and Robert ran to join her. Lucy, who was lingering behind, trying to search every inch of the avenue, arrived just in time to hear Elizabeth saying, 'Look ... look at what I have just found!' She held up a sparkling object in her hand.

Before she could stop herself, Lucy cried out, 'It's my ring! You have found my beautiful ruby ring!'

The other three turned to Lucy in amazement and Elizabeth said, '*Your* ring? Don't be silly! How could a servant girl like you own a ring like this?'

In desperation, Lucy replied, 'But it *is* mine. It was given to me as a present. Please believe me.'

Miss Wade turned and said sternly to Lucy, 'Lucy, that just cannot be true. I must agree with Elizabeth. You could not possibly own a ring like that.' She held out her hand and Elizabeth reluctantly placed the ruby ring in her palm. 'It's very beautiful. It must be worth a lot of money.'

'Please, may I keep it? After all I found it,' said Elizabeth with an air of importance.

'We must ask your mother and father. It is possible that it may have been lost by one of the guests who stayed here in July. As your parents won't be back until Monday, I'll take charge of it until then. I have a small jeweller's box and I'll put it into that to keep it safe.'

Elizabeth was about to protest, but Miss Wade said briskly, 'Now come along and don't sulk. This is something your mother must decide.'

As Lucy followed the others she thought in anguish, 'If only I had gone ahead, I would have found it. And I would be away from here by now. Trust that snake Elizabeth to find it.' Tears welled up in her eyes at the cruel blow that fate had just dealt her. But she forced herself to think positively: 'At least it has been found. That's something. Now I have a chance to get it back. I'll just have to see where Miss Wade puts it and grab it. Lord and Lady Tyrconnell won't be back until Monday, so that gives me a day and a half. Surely I'll have an opportunity before then. Miss Wade may go down to supper to The Room and then I can nip in and get it.'

Entering the nursery again, Lucy hastily set the basket of flowers on the table. When Miss Wade went into her room, Lucy edged around the half-open door and asked, 'Shall I put the flowers in water, Miss Wade?'

Startled, the governess turned from the small drawer in her writing-desk which she had just opened. 'Yes, do, Lucy. You'll find a vase in the brush room. And then go down for the trays. It's almost luncheon time.'

As Lucy put the flowers into water, her thoughts were on her ring. 'At least I now know where it is. I wish I could just run in and take it. But I'll have to be patient. Perhaps when I'm lighting the fires this evening, I'll get a chance.'

Florrie was putting a small blue and white soup tureen on the children's tray. 'Here we are, Lucy. Carrot soup to start, then boiled fowl, mashed potatoes and turnip, with treacle pudding to follow.'

The white cloth had been laid on the table in the schoolroom and the children were waiting, Elizabeth with her usual sullen expression, Robert with his usual friendly smile. Back in the kitchen, Florrie was adding a dish of fried fish to Miss Wade's tray.

Lucy took the tray mechanically and climbed the stairs again. She was deep in thought. The ruby ring was now so tantalizingly near    and yet so far.

## 4    The Sleepwalker

Dinner had already started in the servants' hall when Lucy returned from the nursery.

'It's Prince of Wales soup, roast haunch of mutton, red-current jelly, and baked bread pudding,' Nellie whispered.

'Bread pudding — ugh,' said Lucy under her breath. 'But what is Prince of Wales soup?'

Nellie giggled. 'I asked Mrs. O'Shea the same question. It's turnips mainly. It was invented by a friend of the Prince of Wales, for the poor of the parish. Cheap and nourishing! It doesn't taste bad either. Everything is Prince of Wales now since he was here in the spring.'

There seemed to be more people in the servants' hall than on the previous night. As Lucy looked up to the head of the table she could see the frosty Mr Winters sitting there. She saw him looking her way and turning to Mrs Morris, who was sitting beside him, he made some remark. 'He's talking about me, but I don't care. With a bit of luck I'll soon be gone.' She couldn't resist smiling at him, a smile that was not returned.

'Well, it won't be long now until we have a full house again,' Winters addressed the table. 'And I know that I can rely on all of you,' his gaze flickered over Lucy, 'to maintain that perfection of service for which Langley is justly renowned. I'm sure, Mrs O'Shea,' inclining his head in her direction, 'that your meals will be as perfect as ever. And I know that Sweeney has everything for the shoot under control.'

'Pity we're not having the Lord-Lieutenant this year,' grumbled Mrs O'Shea.

'We will look forward to welcoming Lord Carnarvon next year,' replied Winters.

'I understand you saw the Prince and Princess of Wales in Dublin,' said Ethel.

'Yes, I was privileged to be watching when their carriage passed. A very splendid occasion. They behaved with great dignity, though, as you know, some unseemly incidents marred their visit. I refer particularly to the disgraceful scenes in Cork. Rowdy creatures with placards along the route shouting . . .'

'We'll have no prince but Charlie,' put in Florrie:

> Ah, need I tell it was Parnell,
> Our own beloved Charlie.

Winters fixed her with a frozen stare.

'I don't think we want to discuss Mister Parnell.'

'I understand he's already in the country,' said Mrs Morris.

'Yes. Barnstorming around the towns, calling for an Irish parliament. Home Rule as they call it. Wanting to break our links with the Empire.'

'I thank God I am a loyal servant of Queen Victoria,' said Ethel.

'Yes, indeed. I don't know what the country is coming to. That whole family seem to be subversives. His sisters founding the Ladies' Land League! Inciting rebellion against the proper authorities. Speaking in public, like ... like ...' He was momentarily at a loss for a suitable word.

'So unladylike,' sniffed Ethel.

Mrs O'Shea, Lucy noted with interest, had taken no part in the conversation. Florrie had an angry red spot on each of her cheeks, but after that one interruption, she too remained silent.

The mutton was deliciously tender, and it was stuffed with a savoury mixture of ham and bacon, with herbs, lemon rind and breadcrumbs (Nellie supplied the recipe).

'Who's that?' whispered Lucy to Nellie, nodding at an oldish man with a ruddy face.

'That's old McDyer, the head gardener. And that's Tommy the under-gardener,' discreetly indicating the young man almost opposite them.

'It's all uppers and unders here,' grumbled Lucy. 'There's as much rank down here as there must be upstairs.'

'Not quite!' Nellie's eyes danced with laughter. 'You should hear McGinley on the subject. There was a frightful row in the dining-room one night because his Lordship took in the wife of an earl, while there was a duke's daughter in the party. Oh, not the sort of row Mrs O'Shea and Bella Jane have. Just frosty looks,' and Nellie pursed up her lips and adopted a glassy stare.

After the mutton, the butler, housekeeper and gardener rose and left the table. They were followed by Bella Jane, who, Nellie explained, served them in The Room.

'They take their pudding and tea in The Room. And something a little stronger, I wouldn't be surprised,' she added.

The baked bread pudding, which Lucy had been determined

to resist, turned out to be surprisingly good. The breadcrumbs and milk mixture was flavoured with almonds and candied peel and thickened with eggs. 'That lovely flavour is ... whiskey,' said Nellie. 'When Mrs O'Shea is in a good mood, she throws in a dollop.'

McGinley rolled his eyes at Lucy and made smacking noises with his lips, and Tommy also indicated appreciation.

'At least I can put names on most of the faces now,' thought Lucy.

Dinner finished, Lucy collected the trays and came downstairs again, her arms and legs aching. Back in the schoolroom, Miss Wade said, 'Lucy, you may start the mending now. Everything is in that box over there,' indicating a brightly painted wooden box that stood beside the window.

Lucy groaned inwardly because she hated sewing. They did very little of it in school now, though her mother had shown her how to hem. Lifting the lid of the sewing-box, she found a white frilly petticoat with a large tear in it. Finding a needle and thread in one of the dainty little drawers, she sat down to sew.

'It's good to get sitting down for a while anyway,' she told herself but the afternoon dragged as she sat, head bent over her work, trying in vain to make small neat stitches. Miss Wade and Elizabeth were looking at clothes in Elizabeth's bedroom and when Miss Wade came out and announced that they were going down to the housekeeper's room to see some materials, Lucy's heart rose. Now she could get the ring!

Alas! Robert elected to stay behind, as he was working on some exercises Miss Wade had given him. After a while he stopped and said to Lucy, 'Do you like it here?'

'I've only been here a day,' said Lucy smiling. 'It's not much time to make up one's mind.'

'I know you have a lot of work to do,' Robert sounded concerned, 'and your day is very long. But in time you might become a housemaid and that would be much better.'

'He sounds like a little old man,' thought Lucy, 'but he's nice.'

'You mustn't mind Elizabeth,' went on Robert. 'She can be very trying. That's why the last girl didn't stay. Elizabeth didn't like her so in the end Mamma sent her back home and you were engaged instead.'

'That's what you think!' Lucy wondered how Robert would react if she told him how she really got to Langley.

Robert was still speaking. 'Elizabeth wants to be grown up. She hates being here in the schoolroom with me. She wants to go to parties and always be with Mamma and Papa. But that's not really possible. They're away so much, and even when they're here, there are usually people around. Still, we are allowed down to the drawing-room most days for a little while, and Papa and Mamma often come up to see us, and sometimes they have tea with us here. Next year father says I will be old enough to have dinner with them when there are no guests. As Elizabeth is allowed to do now.'

Lucy digested all this strange information. Imagine not being able to see your father and mother any time you wanted to. The grown-ups seemed to lead a separate life from the children. What an awful way to live! No wonder Elizabeth was so moody. Another thought struck her and she said shyly, 'Master Robert, do you not go to school at all? Will you always be here, doing lessons with a governess?'

'Oh, I've been away at school in England for a couple of years, but I became ill last term so Mamma and Papa decided I should stay at home for the winter and let Miss Wade teach me. I like being home and Fielding and McDyer and Sweeney, the gamekeeper, take me around. I'll inherit all this one day, you know. And I usually ride every day which is great. But I do miss the chaps — Elizabeth is not much fun and she hates playing with me.'

'About as much fun as measles on Christmas Day,' was Lucy's thought. As Robert resumed his work, she began on the sewing again. When teatime came she was glad to put it away and go down for the trays. The children's tea was the same as yesterday. 'They must get sick of bread and butter,' she said to Bella Jane who looked at her in surprise. 'Bring them up plain, that's the idea,' she explained. 'No rich food.' Miss Wade's tea consisted of buns and jam as well as sandwiches and fruit-cake.

In the servants' hall, plates piled high with thick slices of homemade bread and dishes of jam were laid out on the table.

'What kind of jam is this?' Lucy asked Florrie after her first mouthful.

'Greengage jam,' answered Bella Jane proudly. 'Made it a few weeks ago. From the greengages in the kitchen garden. That was the greengage week, that was. Tons of greengages. We were all hard at work. Greengage jam. Compôte of greengages. Preserved greengages in syrup. Dried greengages. Still that lot should see us through the year until next crop.'

'It's delicious,' said Lucy helping herself to more bread and jam.

Tea over and the trays returned to the kitchen, it was time to light the fires. Lucy went to Elizabeth's room first. The fire was slow to light and she blew the reluctant flames until she was red in the face. At long last it got going, and she did the one in Robert's room.

Miss Wade was not in the sitting-room. Was she out? Sometimes, Nellie had told her in answer to her casual enquiry, Miss Wade took a walk about that time of evening, sometimes alone, sometimes with the children. Lucy could only hope that it was one of those evenings. Her heart was thumping as she knocked on the door of Miss Wade's room and she got an awful shock when a voice said, 'Do hurry with the fire, Lucy. It's getting rather chilly in here.'

Lucy's heart sank when she saw the governess sitting at her writing-desk writing letters. Lucy worked as slowly as she could, hoping that Miss Wade would be finished before she

was and decide to go for her walk — twilight had not yet
fallen. But the governess was still writing busily when Lucy
was finished.

'Can nothing go right for me?' thought Lucy in anger. 'I'm
going to have to try later, much later. I'll come back during
the night when everyone is sound asleep.' She shivered a little
at her own daring.

Back in the sitting-room, Robert and Elizabeth were seated
at the table. Robert was working on a jigsaw and seeing Lucy's
interest he showed it to her.

'It's called *Sports and Pastimes* and I've almost finished it,'
slotting another piece into place. Looking at the picture Lucy
saw girls in long dresses and bonnets, dancing and playing
with hoops and sticks. Boys in short sailor jackets and trousers
that fastened at the knee were shooting arrows at a large target
board and playing cricket.

McGinley came in to light the lamps as Lucy stopped to
look at the kitchen Elizabeth was playing with. 'Don't touch

anything,' said Elizabeth sharply, but then added in a softer tone, 'You may look if you like.'

Elizabeth's kitchen opened at the front and had no roof, so that it was easy to see everything. Copper saucepans and ladles of different shapes and sizes hung on the walls, and there was even a tiny sweeping-brush in the corner. The table was set with miniature cups, saucers and plates, and Elizabeth was putting tiny knives and spoons in the right places. 'Well, well, well!' thought Lucy. 'Playing at being Ethel!'

Glancing at the clock on the mantelpiece, she saw that it was a quarter to seven so she went off for the supper trays.

'Here we are, Lucy,' said Florrie. 'Milk soup for Miss Elizabeth and Master Robert — they'll like that.' She poured milk from a saucepan into a dish that contained slices of bread.

'Milk? But it's yellow, Florrie.'

'Aye, that's the egg yolks.'

'Milk soup! Now I've seen everything,' Lucy was thinking as she took the tray off to the nursery.

'Almost ready,' said Florrie when she returned. 'There — chicken pie, sliced tongue and some jam tartlets,' as she placed the last dish on the tray beside the teapot.

The main dish in the servants' hall was mutton pie. 'Always have mutton pie for supper when we have mutton for dinner,' joked Nellie to her. Lucy cut open the crumbly piecrust to discover layers of meat and potatoes, flavoured with onion and herbs. 'Delicious,' she said as she ate it up.

That evening there was very little talk. Everything seemed to be centred on the forthcoming house party. McGinley rose after half an hour and said, 'Time to get the cutlery in order,' and he left.

At the head of the table, Mrs. O'Shea, Florrie and Maggie were pouring over recipe books.

'Give them a nice leg of lamb for the second course, with turnips and a few mushrooms — get Tommy to get us some in the fields. Also, roast ribs with horseradish sauce — his

Lordship is very partial to roast ribs. For the first course, what about mock-turtle soup and grey mullet with anchovy sauce? If we can't get the mullet, we'll have crimped skate with caper sauce? The entrées — vol-au-vent of chicken ... sweetbreads and tomato sauce ... stewed pigeons. Roast grouse for the third course. Then plum tart with whipped cream ... punch jelly ... ices ...'

'How many people are coming?' asked Lucy listening to this litany.

'Six or eight,' replied Maggie.

'They'll never get through that food,' said Lucy.

'That's nothing,' snorted Mrs O'Shea. 'You should have seen the dinners we dished up at the Duke's. Never less than fourteen dishes for the second course. Always three soups. Always ten entrées. Always a choice of twelve desserts, puddings and fruit. And between the entremets and the removes — why at times we ran out of fish and flesh to serve! Take it from me, this is the simple life.'

Lucy went back to the nursery. Perhaps Miss Wade had gone downstairs and the children to bed. No, they were all still in the sitting-room, talking about the guests who would be coming next week. Taking her candle, Lucy went to her room, where she found Nellie sitting on the side of the bed. 'Could you help me with these buttons, Lucy?' asked Nellie.

When she saw the scullery-maid's hands swathed in white, Lucy asked in concern, 'Did you burn yourself?'

'No, me hands get so red and chapped from all the scrubbing that Mrs O'Shea has to cover them in mutton fat and then put on white muslin. There's an awful lot of work when there's anyone coming. Every pot has to be scoured and polished. And all those big covers to keep the food hot. I think it's the sand does it ...'

'Sand?'

'Yes, the pots are cleaned with ale, soft soap and silver sand. Hard on the hands I can tell you.'

'Does the mutton fat help?' asked Lucy.

'Aye, it soothes them all right. Anyway, they'll get a bit of a rest tomorrow. It's Sunday.'

'What happens on Sunday?'

'Nothing much. We have to go to Mass in the morning. Nobody does anything most of the day and we have cold meals — not much cooking. It's as dull as ditchwater. Luckily, I have the afternoon off. If it wasn't for Sunday, I'd never have got off because of all the work for Monday evening. Mrs O'Shea is in a right rage about it, I can tell you. Says house parties should never start on a Monday. Anyway, I'm glad ... I'm going to see the Boyles.'

'Who are the Boyles?'

'People who've been very good to me. They took me in and gave me a roof over me head. Paddy Joe Boyle is a herdsman on the estate and he helped to get me this job.'

Lucy would have liked to hear more but Nellie's face had again taken on that closed private look. Lucy wondered where she had been living before the Boyles took her in.

Anxious though Lucy was to hear Nellie's story, however, she hoped she would go to sleep quickly so that she could go back to the nursery. Luckily, soon the sound of Nellie's gentle snoring reached her, but to her dismay she found herself getting drowsy. She forced herself to stay awake, with thoughts of home and Mum and Dad and David. So she lay, until she felt it was safe to light her candle and make her way downstairs.

Nellie stirred but did not wake as Lucy crept quietly to the bedroom door, which opened with just a slight creak. Moving lightly along the corridor, her bare feet already cold, her long nightdress making a slight flapping noise around her legs, the candle casting eerie shadows, she felt alone and afraid. Quietly she slipped down the back stairs. The lamps had been turned out long ago and poor Lucy's knees were trembling by the time she reached the floor below. As she came through the door on to the carpeted corridor, she took a hasty look to right and left. She jumped, barely suppressing a scream when by the flickering candlelight she saw someone crouching in the window. Beads of perspiration broke out on her forehead as she waited for the figure to challenge her. But it did not speak, so gathering her courage she took a few steps towards it. She sighed with relief when she realised it was only the tall flower-pot with the bushy fern.

Lucy tip-toed along the dark corridor and when she came to the nursery door, she rubbed her clammy hand on her nightdress before slowly opening it. Thankfully it opened silently and she carefully made her way across the room to Miss Wade's door. Listening intently she could hear nothing, so saying a silent prayer she turned the handle and slipped into the room.

Noiselessly setting the candlestick on the writing-table, she started, very gently, to ease open the small drawer.

Suddenly there was a cry from the bed, 'Who is it? Who's there? Elizabeth, Robert, are you ill?'

Panic-stricken, Lucy's hand froze and she could not will herself to open the drawer further. When she heard the rasp of a match from the bedside, she knew there was no escape. She quickly grabbed her candlestick and stretching her arms out stiffly in front of her, she headed in the direction of the fireplace.

By now, Miss Wade was out of bed and coming towards Lucy, who did not allow her gaze to wander. When she reached the fireplace, she placed the candlestick on the hearth and knelt down as the governess reached her.

'Good gracious, Lucy, what are you doing?'

Keeping her eyes wide open, Lucy stared fixedly ahead and said nothing.

'Oh, the poor child,' said Miss Wade. 'She's sleep-walking. She must be worrying about lighting the fires.'

Gently, she raised Lucy to her feet and placing her candle

in her hand, she led her through the sitting-room — and back upstairs again.

Lucy found it difficult to keep a vacant expression on her face and had to fight to keep back the tears that welled up, but at last she was in bed. Sighing, she turned and closed her eyes. Miss Wade quenched the candle, and silently left the room.

'I was so close to getting it,' Lucy thought in despair. 'Another few minutes was all that I needed. Well, I'll just have to try again tomorrow. Surely there'll be another chance.'

She did not have long to dwell on her sorrowful plight. Worn out by the events of the day and the nervous tension she had felt, she was soon fast asleep.

## 5 Nellie's Story

When Lucy woke up and looked at the clock, she jumped out of bed in horror. Shaking Nellie by the shoulder, she said urgently, 'Quick! Get up! Look at the time ...'

Nellie turned over and gave her a sleepy look. 'Did I forget to tell you? We sleep late on Sunday ...'

Miss Wade was already awake when Lucy came to her room with the hot water and spoke pleasantly to her. She did not refer to the midnight visit.

When she had delivered breakfast to the nursery, Lucy came downstairs again to the kitchen. Mrs O'Shea, resplendent in brown twill and a brown hat with feathers, was sitting at the table in a gloomy mood. 'All that work to be done, and so little time.'

'We have all day today,' said Lucy.

'Sunday? There's not much work done round here on Sunday! I'll have to get another pair of hands and that's certain ... Well it's time we got ready for Mass. Lucy, look slippy. Get your brown dress and cloak and bonnet.'

When Lucy and Nellie came back, a horse-drawn sidecar was waiting at the entrance to the servants' courtyard. The household staff, all dressed formally with cloaks and bonnets and highly polished boots, were taking their places.

'Do we really have to get up on that thing?' asked Lucy in horror. 'That thing' was a back-to-back car, with four seats on each side.

'Don't worry,' said McGinley. 'I'll land you up — it's not as high as it looks. Just think what a great view you'll get of the countryside on such a lovely day!'

Lucy allowed herself to be lifted up beside Nellie. The others on her car were Mrs O'Shea, Florrie, Maggie, Minnie, Mary Kate and McGinley.

As they jogged along the country roads to the little town of Dundara, Nellie answered her stream of questions.

'Yes, we are going to St. Catherine's. The others — Miss Wade, Mrs Morris, Winters, Ethel, Bella Jane — go to the C of I. They're luckier — they get the small carriage.'

'What's the C of I?'

'Church of Ireland, silly.'

'What about all the rest of the staff?'

'Fielding and the outdoor staff?' They go by themselves. Walk I suppose.'

It was a beautiful autumn day and the great trees of the estate, for they were still circling it, behind the ribbon of golden stone wall, shone red and yellow and bronze against the brilliant blue sky. They left the estate behind and a sharp turn in the road brought them to the summit of a small hill. Below them lay the town of Dundara and beyond it the blue waters of Lough Dara. It was a tiny village, with the twin spires of

the two churches the most dominant feature of the landscape.

In the chapel, Lucy settled herself down as comfortably as she could on the hard wooden bench — Nellie had told her that there was usually a long sermon.

'That's Father Gallagher,' whispered Nellie as a tall gaunt man mounted the steps of the pulpit. 'You should hear him preaching during Lent. Hell-fire and all.'

A glare from Mrs O'Shea silenced her and Lucy half listened to the various notices of deaths and forthcoming services. Then suddenly her wandering attention was caught when Father Gallagher thumped the pulpit.

'Michaelmas day is almost upon us. And what does Michaelmas mean? Gale day! Times have been hard and there are many here who will have a struggle to pay the rent. There are many indeed who will be struggling to pay an unjustly increased rent. To those I say, "Take heart!"

'A month ago, in Cork, Tim Healy gave this advice: Combine together. Name two or three people you trust. Give to them the rent you think is fair. Let them bank it. The landlord will give in; if not you will have funds to fight him. Funds to help the evicted . . .

'And if anyone should take the land of an evicted man, you have the solution! A non-violent solution. Treat him like a leper of old. Give him no food or drink. Let his crops rot in the ground. Show him — in the streets, at the shop counter, at the fair and in the market-place — your detestation of his crime. And if he enters a place of worship — leave it . . .

'Ostracise him! Isolate him! Boycott him!'

'Did he mean the Tyrconnells?' asked Lucy on the way home.

'No. They're fair landlords. He was talking about Lord Olphert — he owns a lot of the land around here.'

'The best landlord is good for nothing,' Florrie, who had overheard Nellie, said shortly. 'We want the land and we're going to get it.'

'Now, Florrie, calm down,' said McGinley.

'The Canon isn't going to like the bit about leaving the church in a body,' giggled Minnie.

'Pour soul. He's been listening to Father McFadden.' Mrs O'Shea sounded gloomy. 'And no good is going to come of it. Maybe things are different down in Cork. All it's going to mean here is eviction. Might as well tie your guts around a whin bush and pull ...'

When Lucy brought up the luncheon tray, the children were sitting at a small table near the window, taking some wooden animals out of a box.

'No lessons today,' she said cheerfully, as she set the table. There was minced chicken in white sauce and tapioca pudding. 'You'll be able to do another jigsaw.'

'No, not on Sunday. We're only allowed to take out the Ark on Sunday, because it is part of the Bible.'

'Who are these?' Lucy asked, pointing to some carved figures that Elizabeth was taking out of the brightly painted boat-house.

'This is Mr and Mrs Noah,' said Elizabeth with a smile. 'And these are their three sons — Shem, Ram and Japhet.'

'She is pretty when she smiles,' decided Lucy.

'Come, children,' said Miss Wade. 'We mustn't let the food get cold.' As they sat down, she said to Lucy, 'Lucy, you may have the afternoon off. I know this is unusual as you have only been with us a few days. But you have worked very hard ... and I understand you're going to have to work even harder for the next few days.' Her eyes twinkled. 'Mrs O'Shea has asked that you give Nellie a hand in the kitchen because of the house party. I know your home is too far away to visit ...'

'How right you are!' thought Lucy.

'... but you could walk into the village or perhaps Nellie would take you to visit her friends.'

In the servants' hall there was cold meat and treacle pudding.
'Treacle pudding again,' complained Lucy to Nellie.

'Leftovers from yesterday — there's never much cooking
on Sunday,' explained Nellie. 'But there's nothing wrong with
it. You haven't been hungry yet, have you?'

Feeling a little ashamed, Lucy said hastily, 'No, of course
not.' Then, to change the subject, she added, 'Miss Wade is
allowing me the afternoon off.'

Nellie was surprised, until Lucy explained about working
in the kitchen. Then she laughed. 'You'll earn your afternoon,
Lucy, we'll be working until all hours for the next few days.
Always the same when there's company. But never mind that
now. Why don't you come and visit the Boyles with me?'

Lucy accepted the invitation gratefully and hurried off to
collect the nursery trays. She had decided that Miss Wade
was feeling sorry for her on account of the sleep-walking
incident and was giving her a rest from work. But though
she was glad of the chance of getting away from the castle,
even for an afternoon, she was upset that she was missing
a chance to get the ring. Surely the children and Miss Wade
would be doing something for the afternoon. The thought of
the deserted nursery was hard to bear but she was confident
that another opportunity would arise on the morrow.

In her brown cloak she joined Nellie, and as she followed
her along the wide stone-floored passage she realised that there
were even more service rooms than the few she had noticed
the first time she had come along that corridor.

'What's the ice room?' she asked.

'For ice, silly. They collect it from the lake in the winter.
Huge blocks of it. It's stored in an old cave down there and
when we want it in the castle, one of the boys brings it in.
That room faces north and has no window, so it's always as
cold as the north pole.'

Outside the back door, Nellie pointed to a small outbuilding
and said, 'That's the game larder.' Seeing Lucy's puzzled

expression, she explained. 'For pheasant and grouse and hare and things like that. They're always hung where plenty of fresh air can get at them. You see, game has to be hung until it's "high". That means,' she chuckled, 'when the head drops off. The deer are hung in the stables.'

Crossing the courtyard, she went through the archway that led to the stables. Pointing to the right she said, 'The dairy is up that way, but you can't see it from here.'

'What do they do in the dairy?'

'Make butter, of course! The cowkeeper brings in the milk in pails and when the cream separates it's made into butter. They churn on Tuesdays and Fridays, and when the family is in London, the butter is posted to them in oak butter-boxes every Wednesday afternoon. Can't say I'd fancy the life. The dairy-maid is supposed to be hard at work by five in the morning! But you should know all this from your aunt ... now, we go this way.'

She led Lucy around the left side of the stables and through a wide gateway with wrought iron gates. They were closed and padlocked but they climbed over the steps at one side.

Now they were in the open countryside. Nellie set a fast pace and Lucy had to struggle to keep up. It was wild desolate countryside, with a few stunted rowan-trees and the occasional gleam of a moorland lake, though now the landscape was softened with the soft misty bloom of the heather. High blue hills rose around the rim of the horizon.

They came to a narrow stream, beyond which a few scrubby trees grew, and here Nellie agreed to take a short rest. She didn't talk and Lucy was afraid to ask her any questions.

'Come on then, Lucy,' she said in a few minutes and off they set again, hopping on the couple of stepping-stones that allowed them to cross the brook without getting their feet wet. They reached the wood and Nellie, confidently following a much trodden path, ducked beneath the branches of the hazel trees that sprang up behind moss-covered rocks.

Nellie slowed her pace, looking intently at the ground before her. Then gathering her apron she bent down, lifting up pieces of scrub-oak and hazel wood, which she placed in her apron.

'Mrs Boyle is always glad of them for the fire. Maybe you'd gather a few.'

Lucy willingly gathered up her apron and followed Nellie's example.

A shout from Nellie brought Lucy to her side. 'These are even better,' she said as she began putting the circular objects into her apron.

Taking a closer look, Lucy said, aghast, 'But, Nellie, those are cow-pats!'

'Yes, and look how dry they are. They really get the fire blazing,' adding matter of factly, 'The turf are very wet sometimes. Meself and Ned — he's me brother — we used to collect them for our house, right up until the winter we were . . .' Her voice trailed off.

'What happened that winter, Nellie?' asked Lucy gently.

'I'll tell you later,' answered Nellie.

By now the two girls had left the wood and the land grew even more desolate. The purple of the heather gave way to clumps of rushes, which grew in ugly profusion, and the prickly whins stabbed at their clothes as they passed.

'We're almost there now,' Nellie said with a smile. 'I love coming here. It always reminds me of home.'

Lucy clambered across the stone ditch behind Nellie and stood for a moment to get her breath back. Down in the hollow in front of her, she could see an old outhouse which seemed to be covered with grass tufts, a large heap of turf to one side. Nellie was heading in that direction, so the Boyle house must be close by. But, wait, there was smoke coming from the roof of the outhouse. Could people actually be living there!

Following Nellie along the rough track, Lucy got a shock when the door flew open and out rushed several children, all shouting, 'Nellie! It's Nellie!'

Nellie hugged the four children, who ranged from a tiny two-year-old to a girl almost as tall as Nellie. Lucy noticed that they were all barefooted.

At the house, a woman was framed in the open doorway. Smoke billowed out from behind her. Lucy could hardly believe her eyes. 'People actually *do* live here,' she thought. Following Nellie's example she dumped her sticks at the side of the house.

'This is Mrs Boyle.' As Nellie introduced her, Lucy's first feeling, as she looked at the lined face, was that she seemed very old to have such young children. Mrs Boyle's black hair was well streaked with grey, but her blue eyes were bright and twinkling, and wiping her hands on her apron she took Lucy's in her own calloused palm.

'Come in, come in,' she said in a friendly way, gently pushing the children aside to allow the two girls to enter.

Lucy walked into the smoke-filled room. When the door was closed the only light came from a small window in one of the walls. Lucy sat gingerly on the three-legged stool that Mrs Boyle pulled out from under the table, and took stock of her surroundings. The floor was of beaten clay and she found it difficult to balance herself as the stool wobbled on the uneven floor.

'How can they live like this?' she thought, as she gazed around at the few meagre pieces of furniture in the room. A crudely made cupboard hung on one wall, and underneath it was something that looked like a mattress, on a wooden frame, with a couple of thin blankets covering it. A table, which was made from rough boards, and a few fir-tree stumps made up the rest of the room's furniture. A doorway, with a piece of old material draped across it, led to another room, probably the bedroom.

Mrs Boyle went over to the fire, adding some of the sticks and dry cow-pats to the sodden turf. Soon there was a steady blaze under the heavy iron pot that hung by a thick black chain from the iron bar overhead.

'The praties will soon be boiled and then we'll eat. If I'd known you were coming, I'd have tried to get a bit of dried fish ...'

'Never you mind about feeding us,' said Nellie. 'We get more than enough. And we're just after our dinner. Here,' she opened the bundle she had carried on her back and spread it out on the table. 'Mrs O'Shea gave me a few bits of cold mutton and there's some of the treacle pudding .'

As the children gathered around and immediately started eating bits of the pudding, Lucy blushed as she remembered how she had turned up her nose at it back at the castle.'

Mrs Boyle shooed them all away and asked Nellie what was happening at the 'big house'.

Nellie told her about the house party and the dinners that would be eaten, and all the scrubbing of pots and pans that that would mean.

Mrs Boyle sympathised, but Nellie said quickly, 'Isn't it better than the workhouse or the hiring fair?'

'Aye, that it is,' said Mrs Boyle with feeling. 'Poor Dick

has had a hard time of it up north, but at least he's getting fed — or I hope he is. He'll soon be home again and that's an extra mouth to feed.'

The workhouse. Hiring fairs. These were things Lucy had heard her grandfather talk about when he was alive. Stories that had been passed from generation to generation. Stories of a people's poverty and humiliation, but also of their great courage and of their humour. How strange to find herself in a world where they were a living reality.

Mrs Boyle lifted the iron pot from the fire and drained the water from the potatoes outside the door. Then she dumped them into a basket woven from sally branches. There were only three plates, so the younger children ate their potatoes from their hands. Nellie and Lucy refused the offer of food but accepted a cup of buttermilk each.

Nellie and Mrs Boyle chatted away as they ate the simple meal; about neighbours, who had gone to America, who had been taken to the workhouse, who had died, who had been born. Then Nellie said regretfully, 'We'd better be getting back, Lucy.'

Lucy said her good-byes to Mrs Boyle and all the children, who waved after them as they went back up the stony track. When they reached the top and turned to give a final wave, Nellie said, 'Follow me. I want to show you something.'

A quarter of a mile up another track they came upon the ruins of a cottage. Only the foundations remained and some of the stones were covered with nettles and young saplings.

'This is my home,' said Nellie. 'The front door used to be here. This was where the window was. I mind well sitting there, looking out towards the rowan-tree.

The tree, a few bright orange berries shining against the rusty leaves, was still there. But what had happened to the cottage? Lucy turned a shocked face towards Nellie.

'Eviction,' said Nellie in a dull voice. 'It was a fierce hard winter. We had a cow and it died, and the baby was very

sick. The potatoes went bad in the ground that autumn and there was hardly anything to eat. We knew we would have a struggle to pay the rent — and then the agent raised it. The landlord wanted this bit of land, to put sheep on it. So he was glad of the chance to get us out.'

'Was it the Tyrconnells?'

'No. His Lordship wouldn't do a thing like that. It was another family. They lived all the time in London, but they were greedy for every penny they could get out of the land here.'

'What happened?' Lucy asked. She had read about Captain Boycott and evictions and here before her was someone who had suffered that terrible experience.

'It was terrible. The agent came along with the police and a gang of fellows with crowbars. They warn you they're going to knock down the place and out you have to get. I can still see me father carrying our bits and pieces outside. When one of the constables went to help him, me father wouldn't let him touch anything... I thought me mother would never stop crying, and that set the wee ones off. Ned and meself, we just stood and watched, not wanting to believe our eyes. Me father said we'd better go to the Cunningham estate, where his sister Annie lived. It was a long walk, and everyone had to carry something. A neighbour came along with a donkey and cart and he took the bigger things. There we were, in the cold of winter, out on the road, carrying what was left of our home with us.'

'Oh, Nellie, what a dreadful thing to happen. It shouldn't be allowed. Why did nobody object?'

'What could anyone do? The landlord owns the land and if tenants don't pay the rent or he wants the land, out you go. They talk about such things up at the castle sometimes. Florrie says that Father McFadden and Parnell will change all this. But I'm not so sure. Nothing helped us. There'll always be landlords, and they'll always have the power to turn people out of their house as the notion takes them.'

'But, Nellie, things are going to get better. I know they are.'

'Lucy, it's a good thing you can still hope, but sure you're only a child ... what would you know about it? Now we'd better get back or Mrs O'Shea will be evicting us.' There was the ghost of a smile on her lips.

As they walked back to the castle, Lucy ventured to ask, 'Nellie, what happened after the eviction?'

'We stayed with me aunt and a few of her neighbours, until the spring. Then Aunt Annie gave us all her money to help pay the passage to America. I was sick, Lucy; the fever. It was terrible. And they said I couldn't go with them. When they got to America, me father was to send the money for herself and me to follow when he had it earned. But it never came. Lucy, I get afraid when I hear them talking about the awful state some of the ships are in, and that far too many are crowded together, so that if one of them gets sick they all get sick. Sometimes I think they're all dead and that I'll never see any of them again.'

'But why didn't you stay on with your aunt?'

'She got the fever later and she was very very sick. We knew she was going to die. Two of the neighbours used come in and help. I overheard them one day, deciding what to do with me. It was to be the workhouse or the hiring fair in Letterkenny. I heard me father talk of the hiring fairs often. Girls and boys, some of them only nine or so, sent off to work for big farmers, working until all hours, with bad food and not a proper bed to lie in most of the time. Treated like slaves and all for a few shillings. Not all of the farmers are slave-drivers, of course, but I wasn't going to take that risk.

'And I knew if I went into the workhouse I'd never leave it again. So when I got up one morning and found me aunt dead, I took to the roads right away. I remembered that Paddy Boyle worked at the castle and I walked all the way back to him — two days it took me. He brought me down to Mrs O'Shea and she took me on.'

Lucy looked at Nellie in admiration. She had been through so much, and yet she was always so cheerful and pleasant.

Mention of the coffin ships worried Lucy. She had heard about them and of the deaths of many of the Irish emigrants who had sailed in them. She said nothing, but she wondered if Nellie might not be right. Surely if they were still alive, the family would have sent for her. She shivered as she thought of the life of hard work and loneliness stretching ahead.

When they got back to the kitchen, Robert was sitting at the table talking to Mrs O'Shea. He was eating buns and damson jam and before him was a plate of fruit-cake. 'Well,' thought Lucy. 'So this is how he gets round the bread-and-butter regime!'

Maybe if he was in the kitchen, Miss Wade and Elizabeth might also be out of the nursery. She was edging away, on the pretext of hanging up her cloak and seeing to the fires, when Robert said, 'You needn't worry about the fires, Lucy.

Maggie did them when she brought up the tea trays. You see, Miss Wade and Elizabeth are getting out all her clothes for the house party.'

Lucy, her hopes dashed yet again, thought grimly, 'Well, at least they didn't ask me to do any sewing. That petticoat must have convinced them I can't sew!'

'How are the Boyles?' asked Robert of Nellie.

'Great, Master Robert, Paddy Joe wasn't there but they're all in good health, thanks be to God.'

'We rode over that way about a fortnight ago. Their home is in very bad shape. I will try to get Papa to do something about it. He's coming home in the morning.'

Then he left the kitchen.

## 6    Echoes of the Past

Supper in the servants' hall was a rather muted affair. Nellie explained that some of the servants had an early meal and went to evening service. Tonight Mrs O'Shea presided over a table of Minnie, Florrie, Maggie, Becky, Nellie and Lucy. Maggie dished them up mutton collops, which were fried on the pan and served with a sprinkle of herbs and lemon juice. 'I must remember that,' Lucy said to herself. 'It's so quick and tastes so good.'

When supper had been cleared away, Mrs O'Shea said, 'I think we might start the preparations. After all, if we're sitting round the table, it hardly qualifies as work, does it?'

'She means Ethel is out of the way,' whispered Nellie to Lucy. 'She's the one that's really strict on Sunday work!'

'Where's McGinley tonight?' asked Lucy.

'Oh, he'll be hard at it, all by himself, polishing the plate and the cutlery and all that.'

On the kitchen table, Florrie and Maggie were assembling quantities of suet, ham, bacon, parsley, lemon rind and nutmeg for forcemeat.

'Now, remember I want all that real fine, so that it'll go through the mincer in jig time. And don't put in the herbs until tomorrow or it'll spoil ... Maggie, take in that calf's head and scald it... Lucy, give Nellie a hand ...'

Maggie went out to the meat larder and soon came back with a calf's head which, to Lucy's horrified amazement, she plunged into a pot of boiling water.

When she went into the scullery, where she found Nellie sitting beside two large buckets, filled to the brim with pink-skinned potatoes, she asked, 'What do they do with that poor calf's head?'

'For mock turtle soup. They scald it, take the skin off, remove the brain, tie it up in a cloth and simmer for about an hour.'

'How dreadful!' thought Lucy. Nellie grinned at her. 'Well, it's dead, isn't it? Doesn't feel a thing. And the soup is real nice ... but come on,' handing Lucy a knife, 'We've got to peel all these. At least they're already washed.'

'Who does that?' asked Lucy.

'Patrick, the odd-jobs man. He's just left the buckets.'

'Do you have to do this every day?' asked Lucy as they started to peel.

'Most days. Sometimes it's jacket potatoes and then it's just scrub them. If Patrick is busy elsewhere I have to wash them as well. But it's when there are house guests that things are the worst.'

They could hear Mrs O'Shea's voice from the kitchen.

'Harking back to the good old days when she had a staff of fifteen under her,' giggled Nellie.

'... Mind you, you'd never take him for a Duke. Most of the time he went around in old clothes. Used to drive Methers, that was the steward, into fits. "Why?" the Duke used to ask. "It doesn't matter how I dress in the country, because everyone knows who I am. And it doesn't matter how I dress in London, because nobody knows who I am!" That shut up old Methers. Though, mind you, when it came to a full-scale dinner or a big ball, he always dressed to the nines. Decorations, everything. He looked every inch a Duke.'

'Was he very rich?' asked Maggie.

'Rich as Cro-sus, or whatever his name was. The style was something. When we went from Grosvenor Square in London to Ashford Park in Kent, we travelled in two sets of carriages. The first set took us half way. Then we changed into the second set for the rest of the journey. You see the style was quite different in town and in the country...' Raising her voice she shouted into the scullery. 'How's the work, girls...? Go to it with all your might...'

'Funny when you think of it,' said Florrie. 'Compare the old Duke and his riches with Lady Augusta for whom I used to work. Poor as a church-mouse. Yet they're all gentry.'

'She must have had some money,' said Mrs O'Shea.

'Not a penny. Used to have a page-boy's livery. You should have seen it? Lady Tyrconnell would have had it burned. The page-boy always had to fit the suit. So when the present one grew out of it, she used to drive round town looking for a boy that fitted it. Her greatest boast was that she could live on £200 a year.'

'Did she then?' Mrs O'Shea sounded interested.

'Promised to give Squire Mullins the secret but never got round to it. She saved money on everything. Once she wanted to bring some statues over from Italy — left to her by an old cousin. So she sent a telegram to the castle: "Ellis dead home Tuesday kill a sheep". There was no Ellis of course, but she got the cheap telegram rate and as people heard that there was a bereavement in the family nobody searched her luggage.'

'Didn't she marry at the age of eighty?' asked Maggie.

'Yes, for the third time. Someone asked her why. "Always like to see a man's hat hanging in the hall," she said.'

Mrs O'Shea snorted. 'Why didn't she just hang a hat in the hall? Save herself the bother of having a man about the place ... Youngsters, how are you getting on?'

'Just finished,' said Nellie. The tops of Lucy's fingers had grown sore from holding the knife and she sighed with relief as they swept up the peelings and gave the potatoes a wash in the sink before piling them back into the buckets.

'Fill the buckets up with water, and leave them there — it's cool enough,' ordered Mrs O'Shea. 'Then come in to the fire — you can shred some horseradish at the table.'

'It's all very interesting, listening about life long ago,' thought Lucy. 'But come tomorrow, I'll be a hundred years away from here.' She tried to concentrate on the horseradish but her mind was miles away.

Tomorrow! She knew she would get the ring back tomorrow. There had to be a time when Miss Wade, Elizabeth and Robert would leave her alone in the nursery wing. And then it would only be a matter of seconds before she got the ring and twisted it twice on the middle finger of her right hand ...

McGinley appeared noiselessly at the kitchen door. 'Just brought you the paper, Mrs O'Shea,' he said. 'Won't be as quick from now on.'

'Lord Tyrconnell gets the paper,' Nellie said to Lucy. 'And when the family have finished with it, it goes down to Winters. Then to Mrs Morris and then to Mrs O'Shea.'

Mrs O'Shea, who was having the final cup of tea of the day, opened the paper.

'My, oh my!' she said to herself.

'What is it?' asked Florrie.

'Adair is dead. Well, well, well!'

'Who is Adair?' Lucy was about to ask, but Mrs O'Shea, not heeding that the paper had slipped to the floor, seemed to have gone into a trance.

'I never thought I'd live to see the day,' she said finally, picking up the paper. 'John George Adair! Justice of the Peace for Donegal. The Scot who bought Glenveagh ... I remember it as if it were yesterday.' Mrs O'Shea's face had a stricken look about it, most unlike her usual bustling self.

'Glenveagh is north Donegal, isn't it?' asked Lucy.

'Gleann Beithe,' my father told us. 'The Glen of the Silver Birches. Bought land there about thirty years ago. There was trouble from the start. About shooting rights. About rents. And his agent, Murray, was murdered a few years later. So Adair decided to get rid of the tenants. He called them together and told them this was their last rent day — he was clearing the land. That was in December ... just five days before Christmas ...

'Next April the evictions began. I had just got married and I was home at the time — my family lived near Lough Barra. And that was where the eviction gang gathered. Two hundred policemen with bayonets and the crowbar brigade...

'They went first to the house of a poor widow with seven children and levelled the cabin to the ground. I'll never forget the screams and the lamentations — even the police were moved to tears.

'But they carried on. I saw one old man kissing the doorpost of his home as if he would never see it again — and indeed neither did he. I saw men, women and children running to and fro, carrying out their possessions. I saw them trying to enter the houses as they were being levelled. I saw them that night crouched in small pathetic huddles around turf fires in the bushes nearby.'

'What happened them?' asked Lucy.

'Forty-seven families were evicted. Some went to relations and neighbours. Some, the utterly destitute, were sent to the workhouse in Letterkenny. Many of them emigrated. A man by the name of O'Grady founded the Australian-Donegal Relief Committee. He collected funds to help the people go to Australia.'

'I was there when they left,' said Florrie. 'Everyone gathered, neighbours, friends, relatives, to see them off on the road to Letterkenny, on the first stage of the journey to Australia. I mind well what happened when they got to the cemetery. They turned aside and went in. They lay on the graves of their families, keening as at a wake. The sound rose up to the mountains and came echoing back to us. At last they dragged themselves away, carrying with them their little tufts of grass and bits of clay, the last reminders of their native land.

'The procession continued on its way and, one by one, the people walking with it fell away, until at last only the emigrants were left...'

'I hear that Father McFadden went with them all the way.'

'Aye, that he did. And on to Dublin too.'

'And now Adair is dead. Of natural causes. Only one description fits him — black as the Earl of Hell's waistcoat.'

'Why did he do it?' asked Lucy.

'I remember reading it. "In the interests of good estate management." He put deer on the land — for shooting. They say the sun never shines in that valley since ...'

## 7   A Cruel Blow

After breakfast the next morning, Lucy was wondering whether
she would be in the nursery or sent down to the kitchen again.
But when she came up to the nursery for the trays, Miss Wade
had an assortment of Elizabeth's dresses laid out on her bed.

'You'll be working here this morning, Lucy,' she said. 'We
must get Elizabeth's wardrobe into shape for the coming of
the guests. Many of them need to be brushed and the muslins
freshened up.'

'If Spencer was here, she would be better,' fretted Elizabeth.

'Well, she isn't.' Miss Wade's voice had an unusual edge
to it and Lucy guessed Elizabeth was making a nuisance of
herself with preparations for the forthcoming house party. 'So
we'll just have to make do with Lucy ... Now, Lucy, these
woollen dresses need brushing all over; this lightweight one
is too delicate for brushing — just rub it over with a fine
cloth. These two dresses here are silk, so be very careful with
them — all they need is a very light rubbing with a piece
of merino cloth — you'll get it in the brush room. The muslins
can be shaken to take out the creases and I think this pale-
blue one will need ironing — bring it down to Becky in the
laundry room.'

'Don't forget the fruit spot on my white cotton,' put in
Elizabeth, pointing to a minute reddish-coloured stain.

'What a fuss-pot,' decided Lucy, as Miss Wade instructed
her, 'Cold soap the stain very carefully, then touch the spot
with a feather dipped in chloride of soda. If you dip it
immediately in cold water, that should remove it.'

'These flowers look rather crushed,' Elizabeth held up a

pretty straw hat with a garland of flowers. 'And I want all my ribbons seen to — look at the creases.'

'I'll do the flowers,' said Miss Wade wearily. 'When you've finished brushing the dresses, Lucy, take these ribbons and spread this mixture on them.' Seeing Lucy looking at the bottle she had just taken from the cupboard, she explained. 'It's a mixture of gin and honey and soft soap and water. Spread out the ribbons and sashes and scrub the mixture in. Then rinse them out well in three changes of water — you'll have to go down to the kitchen for that — and then get Becky to iron them with a very hot iron.'

As Lucy worked away at the clothes in the schoolroom, her thoughts on the nearby ruby ring, she could hear the lessons, which were being conducted in the sitting-room that morning, progressing. They were reading from a history book that morning and for once Elizabeth wasn't answering all the questions. Probably too busy thinking of her clothes, Lucy thought. But weren't the dresses pretty? Lucy particularly admired the pink-and-white checked one and the silk dress

in a greeny-blue colour that reminded her of the sea. The navy and red sailor suit was very smart, and the white dress with its rows of tiny frills, threaded through with pink ribbon, was quite lovely. But they certainly wouldn't have been much use for climbing trees. How Lucy missed her jeans and runners.

A diversion was provided by the arrival of McGinley with an armful of shoes, and Elizabeth rushed to examine them — the patent leather shoes, the boots of kid or varnished leather and the dainty satin slippers.

When Lucy returned from the kitchen with water for the sashes and ribbons, the sound of a carriage was heard on the gravelled driveway.

'It's Papa and Mamma,' shouted Robert. Evidently he had been waiting all morning for just that sound. He and Elizabeth jumped up and begged Miss Wade to let them go down into the hall.

Lucy's heart was beating so fast that she was afraid she would faint. When they all went down, that would be her chance to get the ring. The children ran from the room, but with a sickening sense of disappointment, Lucy realised that Miss Wade was not going with them. When Elizabeth peeped into the sitting-room she had settled herself comfortably in an armchair and was reading a book. She was not going to go down to meet Lord and Lady Tyrconnell. The bedroom door was out of reach! Lucy could have wept.

When the ribbons were almost finished, there was a sudden knock and then Mrs Morris put her head around the door.

'Miss Wade,' she said pleasantly, 'I wonder would you come along with me for a few minutes? I was wondering if we should change the curtains in the blue bedroom. I know it's a little early for changing them, but Fielding says we're going to have a cold snap of weather and they are rather lighter than the others. I'd like your opinion.'

Lucy's poor heart did a double somersault. At last ... at long last ... this was her chance!

Miss Wade came into the schoolroom and asked, 'Are you finished yet, Lucy?'

'Not quite,' lied Lucy. 'I still have two to clean, and then I must take them down for ironing,'

'Well, be as quick as you can — I told Mrs O'Shea we wouldn't keep you long and I'm anxious that you get back to the kitchen as soon as possible.'

'All right,' agreed Lucy. 'I'll only be a minute.'

As the door closed behind the housekeeper and the governess, Lucy dropped the sashes and rushed into Miss Wade's bedroom. With trembling hands she opened the drawer and took out the little box. At last she had the ruby ring within reach!

Suddenly a voice behind her said, 'Lucy, what on earth are you doing here?' It was Robert.

Lucy jumped and in her fright she dropped the box. It opened and the ring rolled out, landing almost at Robert's

feet. Picking it up he stared at Lucy and said reproachfully, 'Lucy, you were going to steal the ring. And I was beginning to like you. I'll have to tell Miss Wade.'

'No, Robert,' pleaded Lucy. 'Please don't. It's my ring. It really is . . . and I only want to hold it for a few minutes. . .'

Still carrying the ring, Robert led the way back into the schoolroom. Lucy followed him, and sitting down, she buried her face in the ribbons that had been so carefully cleaned and burst into tears.

'What's the matter?' asked Robert. 'Lucy, you know that you couldn't possibly own a ring as valuable as this. It may belong to one of the guests who were here in July. Miss Wade has to show it to Mamma, and she has to ask the guests who will be here this afternoon. Now I'm going to put it back in the drawer. Oh, Lucy, please don't try to steal it again.'

When he came back into the schoolroom, Lucy was still sobbing. 'You don't understand. Nobody understands. It *is* my ring.'

Getting up and wiping away her tears, she looked guiltily at the ribbons. She knew she should be taking them down for ironing, but that would have to wait. Her urge to confide in someone was overwhelming and Robert had been so kind to her that it seemed providential that he was there.

'Robert, this may seem strange to you . . . please listen before you say anything . . . but I don't belong to this age at all. I come from the future — 1991 to be exact. My Gran gave me the ring for my birthday. It's a star ruby and a great-uncle of hers got it in India. It's supposed to have magical powers. I made a wish and that is why I'm here. Now I have to get it back to make my second wish — and then I'll be home again.'

She didn't mention just how the wish should be made. She felt she could trust him but what if he wanted to try the ring out? It would work for Elizabeth!

Robert began to laugh. 'Lucy, I know you probably believe

what you've just said. But it couldn't possibly be true. I think
you have a very vivid imagination and maybe you invented
the story to get the ring. It's only an old ring, anyway. Mamma
had plenty and so has Elizabeth. Perhaps I could persuade
her to give you one of hers...'

'Robert,' said Lucy in agony. 'You're not listening. What
I'm saying is true. About not belonging to this age...'

'But you can't *prove* it to me.' Robert sounded doubtful.

'I could ... if I could only hold the ring again. That's all
I ask. Just to be allowed to put it on my finger. I can't steal
it ... you'll be here.'

For a moment she wondered if she should not brush past
him as he stood in the doorway and grab the ring. It was
a tempting prospect. But if Miss Wade returned and caught
her in the act and before she had got the ring, she knew she
would be sent away in disgrace and she would never have
another chance of getting home.

As Robert seemed to be wavering, Lucy made an even more
urgent plea. 'Just let me have a ring for an instant. That's
all I ask. If what I say is true, I'll get my second wish and
be back home. That'll prove that what I'm saying is not just
a story I made up.'

'But what will happen when the others come back and you're
gone and the ring is gone.'

'Tell them that when you came back, there was nobody
here. They'll think I stole the ring and ran away. But that
won't matter to me ... Please, please, Robert.'

As they stood facing each other, Lucy in anguish, Robert
regarding her dubiously, the door to the nursery opened. Miss
Wade had come back.

'Have you not brought down those ribbons yet?' she asked.
'Really, Lucy, it's too bad of you. Here, give them to me.
I'll look after them. Robert, you are to go down to join your
parents for luncheon. Lucy, bring up my tray, get your own
dinner, and help Mrs O'Shea all afternoon. You can come

up after tea and do the fires . . .'

Elizabeth burst into the room, saying in excitement, 'I was telling Mamma about the ring, Miss Wade. She says I'm to bring it down and give it to her. She's going to show it to the guests and if it doesn't belong to any of them, she may give it to me.'

'Well, I don't think she'll give it to you at once — you're much too young. She'll probably hold it in safe keeping until you are older. She may allow you to wear it on very special occasions.'

Elizabeth clapped her hands with glee and threw a triumphant glance at Lucy, who watched as Miss Wade fetched the little box and gave it to Elizabeth. Robert threw Lucy a concerned glance as they passed and then they were gone.

The ring was gone. How would she ever get it back now?

## 8  The Secret Stairs

Lucy was so downcast at dinner that Nellie, suspecting that something had happened but not knowing what, nudged her and told her to cheer up. 'Nothing's that bad,' she whispered. 'You can tell me about it after — if we get a chance to open our mouths — Mrs O'Shea has been planning that much work I don't know how we're ever going to get through it.'

Dinner was a rather rushed affair, and Winters and Mrs Morris took barely twenty minutes over their boiled bacon and cabbage. Lucy could hardly eat a mouthful, and only took a spoonful of her damson pudding.

There were two additions to the servants' hall that day. Seated next to Mrs O'Shea was a rather unctuous-looking man with a domed head, and a carefully arranged hair-do with hair growing down his cheeks. On the right of Winters was a thin severe-looking woman with dark hair, which was parted in the centre, pulled back from her pale face. She wore a dark dress, with a white jabot at the neck. Lucy noticed that she hardly talked at all.

'That's Fox, the valet,' explained Nellie, 'and Spencer, the lady's maid. Tell you about her later.'

Just as they arrived back in the kitchen, there was a sudden flurry in the passage outside, and a tall and rather portly man with a beaming face came in, accompanied by Robert. His skin had a ruddy tinge, suggesting that he spent most of his time outdoors.

Mrs O'Shea dropped the bowl she was about to put on the table, wiped her hands on her apron and said, 'Your Lordship, welcome home.'

107

'Thanks, Mrs O'Shea. And how's everybody down here —
the hub of the house I always say. I'm looking forward to
having some real cookery again. Didn't get a thing to eat in
Scotland! I kept telling them about your haunch of venison
and your grouse and steak pie. Lord Gordon asked for your
name — but I kept that to myself. Didn't want you getting
any offers in the post.' His eyes twinkled. 'And Florrie and
Maggie — as pretty as ever. And Nellie — you've grown,
child. And who is this?' laying his hand on Lucy's head.

'Lucy — she's the new nursery-maid.'

'Well, Lucy, I hope you're very happy with us here . . .
now, Robert, let's go and visit the stables and the gardens.'

As he left, Mrs O'Shea purred, 'A real gentleman.'

'Not like his other half,' sniffed Florrie. 'Can't think how
they ever got together. Talk about fire and frost!'

'She's not that bad,' said Mrs. O'Shea indulgently. 'She can't
help her manner. And of course she doesn't have the
background.'

'What background?' Lucy was curious.

'The English are that much more withdrawn than we are.

Servants are servants to them. Here it's much more friendly
... now that's enough chat. Nellie, you and Lucy had better
start on the vegetables right away. Scrub those artichokes and
make sure there's not a speck of dirt on them, then bring
them back here. And get those carrots ready. Lucy, take these
mushrooms — don't wash them — takes all the flavour out
— just wipe them with a piece of flannel — cut out any bad
parts ... Go to it with all your might!'

McGinley appeared in the doorway. 'Her Ladyship wants
to see Lucy right away,' he announced.

'Lucy? What does she want with Lucy?' grumbled Mrs
O'Shea. 'Don't tell me she's taken to welcoming new staff.
Anyway, Lucy, get along to the drawing-room — and mind
you get back just as quick as you can. You were missing half
the morning when you should have been down here. Don't
be missing half the afternoon or we'll never get done.'

Nellie shot her a sympathetic look as she took off her apron
and washed her hands. With shaking legs she followed
McGinley up the back stairs and through the green baize door
into the hall. 'This is Lucy, your Ladyship,' he said with a
bow, as he left the drawing-room, pulling the double doors
after him. Lucy took a deep breath and advanced into the
room. Elizabeth, who was sitting on a silk-covered chair, eyed
her speculatively.

'You can run along now, Elizabeth,' said Lady Tyrconnell.

'But Mamma ...' began Elizabeth.

'Run along, Elizabeth. You will be sent for when the guests
arrive.' Elizabeth approached and seemed about to throw her
arms around her mother's neck. But Lady Tyrconnell turned
aside and said coldly, 'You'll crush my collar ... there, you've
disarranged it already.'

Elizabeth flushed and went to the door. Lady Tyrconnell
rearranged the lace collar on her dark plum-coloured dress
and turned to Lucy. Looking down at her, Lucy saw a woman
with a pale oval face framed with glossy brown hair which

clustered in curls on her forehead. She would have been beautiful except for her rather petulant expression and thin lips which were now pursed together. As she waited for her to speak, Lucy looked around her.

The drawing-room had a high ceiling which was decorated with flowers and leaves carved in plaster. The carpet, in the centre of the parquet floor, echoed the ceiling decoration. The room was panelled and painted pale cream, the moulding near the ceiling and on the lower part of the walls being picked out in shining gold. A huge chandelier hung from the ceiling and around the walls were landscape paintings in ornate frames. A fire burned in the white marble fireplace. The furniture, in pale yellow silk, seemed almost miniature for the size of the room; there were chairs with curved legs and cabinets and small tables against the walls. The prettiest, Lucy thought, was a black lacquered cabinet, inlaid with beautiful flowers and birds.

Lady Tyrconnell was sitting on a long couch to one side of the fireplace. Eventually she spoke.

'So you are Lucy. What is this extraordinary story I have been told about a ring? Elizabeth has told me you tried to claim it as your own — you, a servant girl. The only way you could possess such a ring would be if you had stolen it. Did you steal it?'

Lucy felt her cheeks getting red as she replied, 'I did not steal it ... I ...'

Before she could say any more, Lady Tyrconnell interrupted her. 'I will be asking my guests if any one of them lost such a ring when they were here at the end of July. If someone claims it, then that is the end of the matter. If no one claims it, the question will be how it got here ...'

'I dropped it,' said Lucy wearily. 'On the avenue.'

'The question will be ...' continued Lady Tyrconnell as if Lucy had not spoken, 'where it came from? We will have to institute enquiries and find out — if, as you say, it is yours

— where you got it. It cannot have been come by honestly.'

Lucy realised the futility of saying anything further so she waited submissively for Lady Tyrconnell to continue. 'My first reaction was to send you home immediately, but Miss Wade, whose opinion I value, said that she was sure it was all a mistake, that you made up the story in order to get the ring, probably not realising its value. But if that is the case, you told a lie. And I will not tolerate servants who lie, especially those who are working near my children ... do I make myself quite clear?'

'Yes, your Ladyship,' said Lucy, thinking to herself that she must at all costs stay near the ring. If she was sent away, she would lose all chance of getting it back. An amusing thought had struck her while Lady Tyrconnell was speaking. Suppose they did send her home. What then? They would discover she didn't have a home! But one look at the cold classical beauty before her banished the thought. Lady Tyrconnell wouldn't have the faintest hesitation in getting rid of her — to the workhouse!

As she returned to the kitchen, Lucy wondered what she would do next. Lady Tyrconnell now had the ring. Where would she put it? Probably in her own bedroom. Lucy's heart sank down to her boots when she realised that, whatever the chances of taking the ring from Miss Wade's room, it would be almost impossible for her to get into the main house — and she didn't even know where Lady Tyrconnell's bedroom was. She was furious with herself for not having made a greater effort to get the ring while it was still in the nursery. Surely she could have thought up some plan. Now her only hope seemed to be Robert. If she could convince him that her story was true — then he would help her.

'And about time too,' groused Mrs O'Shea when Lucy came back. 'What was all that about? Must have been reading you the Bible ... now, go to it with all your might. We've got to get all this up to the drawing-room. The first carriage has just arrived and they'll be looking for their tea.'

Bella Jane and Maggie were rushing around taking scones and cakes from the oven. Mrs Morris was there too, putting the final touches to an elaborate piece of confectionery.

'Here,' said Florrie to Lucy, 'toast these tea-cakes and make sure you don't burn them.'

It wasn't an easy task as there were so many people around the range, but Lucy persevered and managed to get the cakes toasted without burning any of them or getting in anyone's way. Florrie took them from her when they were ready and put them in a muffin dish over a basin of boiling water. Mrs O'Shea was taking honey cake out of the oven and calling to Nellie, 'My snow cake . . . get it at once.' Maggie was decorating plates of cucumber sandwiches with sprigs of parsley.

At last everything had been sent up to the drawing-room, where McGinley, in white gloves, was waiting. 'Winters will have set out the silver — teapot, cream-jug and sugar bowl,' explained Nellie. 'Sometimes her Ladyship pours the tea. But if there's a big crowd, McGinley does it, and Ethel goes around with the food.'

Lucy brought Miss Wade her tea, which included some of the toasted tea-cakes. The governess was all alone, the children having gone down to the drawing-room. 'What a change from bread and butter!' thought Lucy.

'Lady Tyrconnell has spoken to you, I understand,' said Miss Wade. When Lucy nodded, she went on, 'Do try and put the whole thing out of your head. Lady Tyrconnell may seem stern but she is a good employer and we must try and do what she says.'

'Yes, Miss Wade,' said Lucy meekly as she began to light the fires. Miss Wade left her, saying that she wished to see the lady's maid of one of the visiting guests.

'Wouldn't it just happen like this!' said Lucy savagely to herself. 'Here I have the whole place to myself — and what use is it now? I'm here ... and the ring is in the drawing-room.'

As she put her box back in the brush cupboard, she noticed, for the first time, a panel in the wall, with a carved knob in the centre not unlike one she had noticed in the drawing-room. She hadn't noticed it before. It must have been covered up by a wall-hanging which she had pushed aside while looking for the merino cloth.

Curiously she pressed the knob. The panel slid aside and Lucy, peering into the darkness beyond, saw a flight of narrow steps. 'A secret passage!' she thought in delight, wondering if she dared to explore. Would she have the time before Miss Wade or the others returned? Deciding that as the brush room was beside the main door into the sitting-room, she would be able to get out without being seen, she decided to chance it. She got the matches from the sitting-room mantelpiece and lit her candle.

Standing on the top step of the stairs, she pulled the panel closed behind her but did not quite shut it. With heart thumping, she slowly descended the dusty winding stairs, shuddering as what seemed like cobwebs brushed by her face.

When she reached the bottom, by the flickering light of her candle she could see a panel before her. She pushed it gently. At first nothing happened, but the second time she tried it, a narrow section of the panel opened inwards. Breathlessly she peered through the slight opening.

The sound of people talking and laughing came to her quite clearly. She gave the panel another little push and peered out. She was looking into the drawing-room!

Ladies in elaborate tea-gowns of trailing silk and chiffon and bearded moustached men were sitting around, being served by McGinley and an immaculately turned out Ethel, the streamers on her cap bobbing as she passed around the sandwiches and cakes.

'What if they should see me?' thought Lucy, shrinking back into the shadows. Then she realised that the opening was so small that it was unlikely to be noticed, unless the wall was examined inch by inch. She was also reassured to see that the position of the inlaid cabinet, just in front of the moveable panel, meant that nobody could come too close to the wall.

The conversation was interrupted by Lady Tyrconnell, who had just risen to her feet and gone over the mantelpiece. Conscious that she wished to say something, everyone stopped talking.

'I have something in my possession,' she said in her high-pitched voice, 'which may actually belong to one of you. Now, I did not steal it,' a little tinkling laugh, 'my daughter found it the other morning and it occurred to me that perhaps someone in the party lost such a ring while staying here in July.'

Somebody moved in front of the gap in the panel and Lucy deduced rather than saw that Lady Tyrconnell had opened the little box and was showing the ring. There were murmurs of surprise and excitement and the ladies all moved closer to examine the ring. Lucy could hear the comments: 'Beautiful!' 'How it shines!' 'Such a perfect ruby!' But no one seemed to claim ownership, because when the blocking shoulder moved away, Lucy could see Lady Tyrconnell putting the ring back into its box. 'My daughter will be so pleased,' she said. 'She has rather set her heart on it. Now, I'm sure you'd all like to have a little rest before changing for dinner.'

She pulled the long tasselled rope which hung to the right of the fireplace. Mrs Morris entered and the ladies left the room. Lucy wondered if Lady Tyrconnell would take the ring up with her, but, no, she put it into a drawer in a little bureau which stood beside the fireplace. The men soon followed the ladies, one of them talking about having a game of billiards.

Was this to be her chance at last? Lucy could hardly restrain her excitement as she heard the doors close behind the guests. Cautiously, she peered out.

Alas! Winters and McGinley appeared and Lucy heard the butler giving instructions about the fire and the lights. Ethel also came in, to clear away the tea-things and tidy the room. Lucy hastily closed the panel and heard a faint click.

'I'll have to leave it,' she thought. 'Heavens knows how long they'll be there. Still, I know where it is. I'll get it tonight.'

The kitchen was a scene of hustle and bustle. Florrie was stirring a large pot of soup that sat on top of the black range. Maggie was chopping turnips at one end of the table, Mrs. O'Shea was filling small pastry cases with a mixture of chicken and sauce and giving a rapid stream of instructions to Nellie. 'Saucepan four — for the sweetbreads ... two for the pigeons. Hasn't that boy brought in the mullet yet? Florrie, you could leave that soup and start on the sauces ... Lord, love us,' this was when she caught sight of Lucy. 'Where have you been ... and look at the state of you? Here, brush the dust off yourself and give Minnie a hand with the hot water ...'

Looking at herself in the small mirror over the sink in the scullery, Lucy was not surprised at the cook's reaction! Her face was streaked with dust and her cap was all askew. Quickly washing her face and straightening her cap, she hurried back to the kitchen where Minnie was filling cans from the tap of the large copper urn on the right hand side of the range. Handing Lucy two cans, and picking up two herself she said, 'Just follow me, Lucy ...'

Lucy followed Minnie up the back stairs, through the baize door and into the bedroom corridor. 'Just knock on the door,' instructed Minnie, 'and say, "It's your hot water." The lady's maid will come and take the cans. Then we must go down and refill them ... there are four bedrooms to be attended to.'

Lucy knocked at one of the doors which was opened by the thin woman Lucy had seen at dinner. She seized the can and hissed, 'You took your time. Lady Tyrconnell does not like to be kept waiting.'

When they were on their way downstairs again, Lucy said to Minnie, 'That lady's maid, Spencer is it? Is she always like that?'

'Mostly,' replied Minnie cheerfully. 'She thinks herself a cut above everyone here. But she's been sourer than usual lately. Cook says she had been let down.'

Lucy was puzzled. 'Let down?'

'You know . . . deserted by her man friend,' Minnie explained.

'How sad,' said Lucy sympathetically.

'Save your feelings for yourself,' said Minnie darkly. 'Wouldn't give her the time of day, that one? She's a real trouble-maker.'

When they had delivered the second lot of hot water cans, Lucy looked over the landing staircase down to the next landing. The enormous oil lamps that were suspended by chains from the high ceilings were already lighting and a fire was blazing in the fireplace at the top of the stairs. 'One fire isn't much,' she concluded. 'It must get really cold here in winter. No wonder everyone has to have fires all the time.' She was thankful she only had four to attend to. Ethel and Minnie had all the downstairs fires to do as well as the bedroom ones.

She was returning down the corridor towards the baize door when she heard a voice behind her. It was Robert.

'Lucy. Wait a minute!'

'I only have a minute,' said Lucy with a grin. 'Mrs O'Shea will be livid if I don't get down quick. They're all in a fuss about the dinner.'

'Lucy, I've been thinking . . . about what you said. It doesn't make sense, of course . . . but maybe . . .'

'Robert,' said Lucy eagerly, 'all I need is the ring for a few minutes. You will be there, so I can't run off with it. If what I say is true, I will disappear. If it isn't, I give you back the ring and that's the end of it.'

'Oh, Lucy, I want to believe you. But if I take the ring I'll really be stealing it. If only you could prove that what you say is true . . .'

Hearing footsteps on the stairs behind them, Lucy said quickly, 'I'll think of something — and let you know,' and she ran off towards the baize door.

As there were so many visiting valets and ladies' maids, Lucy had been told to help Bella Jane, so after an earlier than usual delivery of the nursery trays, she went into The Room.

It was a cosy room, with armchairs placed on either side of the open fire. The curtains were drawn and the oil lamp threw a soft glow over the snowy white tablecloth. Bella Jane placed the boiled leg of pork over a dish of hot water on the sideboard, and Lucy put the vegetables over another. The room began to fill with people — Winters, Mrs Morris, Fox, Spencer and several unknown faces, which must belong to the visiting servants.

Bella Jane placed the meat in front of Winters and removed the cover. He carved and the plates were handed around by Bella Jane. Lucy followed with baked tomatoes and haricot beans. 'Winter's first, then Mrs Norris, then the visitors on either side, then the rest,' Bella Jane had instructed her. Lucy's hand was not quite steady as she approached Winters, but luckily there were no accidents.

Standing with Bella Jane at the sideboard, except when she was serving, Lucy didn't hear very much of the conversation which was mainly about the prospects of sport on the morrow, the weather and the various parts of Ireland and England that the visiting staff had been to in the past few months. Somebody mentioned the forthcoming election.

'I believe we can rely on Salisbury to uphold the integrity of Empire,' said Winters in a voice that disposed of that topic of conversation.

Half way through the baked lemon pudding, the sound of a gong reverberated through the house. The ladies' maids hastily finished and left the room.

'The dressing-bell,' explained Bella Jane. 'That's about an hour before the dinner-bell.'

When Lucy returned to the kitchen, having collected the nursery trays, the dinner seemed well under control and Mrs

O'Shea was sitting at the table having a chicken pasty, though Florrie and Maggie were still fussing to and fro, watching saucepans on the range, whisking sauces and checking the meats in the oven.

'There's some chicken pie,' said Mrs O'Shea. 'Better grab a little now. Because once dinner starts it'll be all hands on deck. Won't be long now.'

'What are we to do?' asked Lucy, taking a piece of pie.

'Anything you're told. Carry up dishes to the dining-room lift. Take back to the kitchen anything that comes down. And in between, wash everything in sight — pots, pans, saucepans, covers, containers . . .'

Lucy was almost finished when another booming gong sounded. 'That's the dinner-gong,' said Nellie. 'That's the signal for them all to assemble in the drawing-room.'

Ethel, who had just come down to the still-room for some more preserved ginger, looked into the kitchen, dish in hand. She smiled at Lucy. 'Would you like to see the dining-room?' she asked. 'It's all set up and there's nobody there at the moment. The ladies will be gathering in the drawing-room.'

'Love to!' Lucy slipped off her chair and looked appealingly at Mrs O'Shea.

'Well, a quick look, that's all,' she grumbled, adding to Ethel, 'Every time I send that one anywhere she's always away an hour. So mind you're back before Winters announces "Dinner is served." Well before it!'

All the chandeliers in the dining-room were lit and the table looked magnificent, with gold-edged plates, shining silver cutlery and crystal glasses. Down the centre of the table, interspersed with low flower arrangements, tall tazzas contained an assortment of fresh and dried fruit. The centrepiece was a tall tazza with luxuriant bunches of grapes, apples, plums, and pears, clustered around a magnificent pineapple.

'It's beautiful,' breathed Lucy, and even Winters, in full and splendid evening suit and busy at the sideboard where

the wines had been laid out, permitted himself a genial smile at her obvious admiration.

The walls of the dining-room were covered with dark red damask and hung with sombre portraits of ladies and gentlemen in costumes which ranged through the centuries. Lucy particularly admired a beautiful lady who was dressed in a pale-grey satin dress, the stiff folds shimmering with highlights.

'That's Lord Tyrconnell's grandmother,' whispered Ethel. 'Her parents objected to the marriage, so they eloped one night. That's her husband, over there.'

'Are they all ancestors?'

'All! And always hung in the dining-room. The tradition was to dine with your ancestors . . . Quick, the ladies are coming down . . .'

Lucy went to the half-closed door of the dining-room, through which she could see the procession descending the main stairs. The first was a tall auburn-haired lady, her hair

piled high on her head, wearing a narrow-skirted dress of green satin; the bodice was a deep cream with pale-green embroidery, and draped around her shoulders was a cream shawl appliqued in green. 'That's Lady Gordon,' whispered Ethel.

Lucy had hardly time to recover from her admiration when two more ladies appeared — a dark-haired lady in a dress of deep red velvet ('The Countess of Rossmartin,' filled in Ethel), with a bodice of lighter red satin and a deep fringed black shawl with delicate floral embroidery. The other lady ('The Honourable Mrs Fitzgerald,' supplied Ethel) was blonde; her dress fell straight from the shoulders at the back, with sleeves puffed at the shoulders, and the soft colouring of pink and green flowers on a white background was echoed in her shawl.

Last came Lady Tyrconnell, and Lucy thought she outshone the other ladies as the moon outshines the stars. She wore a dress of delicate black lace mounted over cream satin, and in her upswept hair a plume of feathers was fastened.

'She had that dress made for the Viceregal ball last winter,' Ethel told her. 'The Lord–Lieutenant requested that all the ladies wear dresses of Irish manufacture. That lace was made by the nuns in Carrickmacross. You should have seen it before it was mounted — it was as fine as a cobweb.'

The kitchen was at crisis pitch, with everyone flying around. Lucy helped Nellie to bring dishes to a rather primitive lift which was raised by pulley to the passage outside the dining-room. 'Minnie is at the other end, and she'll hand the dishes into the dining-room. You saw the screen at the back of the room. There is a table behind it and Winters will be there, putting any last-minute touches to the dishes — they are kept hot over big dishes of boiling water. When the soup is finished, the next course is set on the table, and McGinley and the other footman will help everyone.'

'The other footman?'

'Remember the sallow-faced man who came into the scullery

with the potatoes? That's him. He's really the odd-jobs man
— cleans riding boots, carries in coal and potatoes. Sometimes
he serves in The Room and when there is company they put
him in livery and he becomes a footman! He's called Patrick
— and he's a cool customer . . .'

Lucy hadn't time to ask her what she meant as it was time
to load up the next course.

It was hard work and Lucy was exhausted when the puddings
had been served and she and Nellie staggered back to the
kitchen with the last lot of dirty dishes.

Mrs O'Shea was sitting at the kitchen table, a mug in hand.
Nellie said with a grin, 'She'll calm down now once the dinner
is over.'

'Well, I think that all went well,' Mrs O'Shea was saying
to Florrie. 'The ribs were done to a turn — just the way his
Lordship likes them.'

'Can't understand how they can eat meat with blood
practically dripping from it.' Florrie wrinkled her nose in
disgust.

'That's the way they like it. Down here, everyone wants
it done to a cinder. And look at all the things they eat up
there — hare, venison . . . even rabbit. I'd like to see Winters
eating rabbit. "Vermin," he calls it . . . Now, girls, you'd better
start on the wash-up.'

'Two minutes,' pleaded Nellie. 'We've been run off our feet
all night.'

'Sure, aren't you young and able to stand it? And you've
every modern comfort. In my young days here the dining-room
was half a mile away from the kitchen. Cook used to dish
up the food and James the footman would literally run with
it to the dining-room. All along the corridor and up the stairs
— that was in the old house.'

'It must have been cold by the time it got there,' suggested
Lucy, wanting to prolong the conversation.

'Of course it was! On a cold night it turned stone cold before anyone could get it eaten. You're lucky living in this day and age, with all the conveniences we have now.'

Lucy's thoughts drifted away. 'If only I could get Robert on my side. Then he'd help me to get the ring back. I must work out a plan.'

More cheerful now, she followed Nellie through to the scullery, with its two delph sinks set in wooden frames, and heavy, ugly, brass taps. Copper and iron saucepans and stewpans sat on the floor, and various containers of earthenware were piled up on the draining-board.

'Lucky, did Mrs O'Shea say?' groaned Lucy as she helped Nellie to pour the large pot of boiling water they had brought from the kitchen into the scullery sinks. 'We'll be here all night.'

'So the sooner we start the better!' Nellie handed over a cloth and a brush, and lifting a copper saucepan from the floor she started scouring it out. 'At least we don't have all the fiddley things to do. Poor Ethel and Minnie will be hard at work in the butler's pantry upstairs, washing all the china and glass. And woe betide them if they break a single thing!'

'I don't know which is the hardest work,' moaned Lucy, rubbing at a particularly obstinate stain. 'What happens to all the left-over food?'

'Florrie and Maggie will be clearing away now. Some of the food goes into pies and hashes for the servants' hall and The Room tomorrow, and the cold meat and game will appear on the sideboard for breakfast upstairs.'

'Where's it all kept?'

'In the dry larder up there.' Nellie nodded her head to the three steps that led from the kitchen. 'It's cool . . . gets lots of air.'

'What wouldn't they give for a fridge,' mused Lucy. 'But they'd have to have an enormous one to take all the food that came back down from the dining room.'

They finally got through the last of the containers that Florrie and Maggie had cleared and the scullery was now as clean as a new pin. Back in the kitchen Maggie was scrubbing the wooden table and cleaning the oven. Mrs O'Shea took another swig from her mug and began on more stories of the olden days. Of dukes and duchesses, of balls and soirées, of shooting parties on the Scottish borders, of the one time she had been to the south of France . . .

Lucy listened with half an ear; a daring plan was forming itself in her mind.

McGinley was in the kitchen now. 'Brought down a special message from his Lordship. They're singing your praises in the dining-room — as usual.'

'And why wouldn't they. I'll bet that was the finest meal they've had since the last time they were here . . . Now, girls, off to bed. I'll need you early in the morning. Florrie, get them a couple of pies — I think they deserve them.'

By the light of the candles they were carrying, Lucy could see that the walls of the dry larder were tiled in white and that the wide shelves that ran along the walls were covered with plates and dishes containing pies, joints of meat and poultry, most covered with domed perforated covers, jellies and tarts. Florrie withdrew two pies and the girls went wearily to bed.

## 9 Midnight Vigil

As they ate their pies, Lucy was still thinking about the ruby ring, and the plan she had decided upon. She must go downstairs tonight, using the secret staircase, and into the drawing-room. She knew where the ring was. It would only take her a second to get it. And then!

'What time will the guests go to bed?' she asked.

'About eleven or twelve, I think. They don't keep late hours when they're shooting next day.'

Lucy looked at the clock; it was just after eleven. Nellie, already undressed and in bed, said with a great yawn, 'I'm that tired I could sleep till Ladyday. We should have gone to bed earlier instead of listening to Mrs O'Shea and her stories. Sure, what's the good of going over the past. Everyone says how terrible things were ... and the evictions go on — I should know. Take my advice and go to sleep now or you'll never be able to get up in the morning.'

Lucy hardly heard what she was saying. Could she risk it? The nursery was apart from the main house so there was little likelihood of meeting anyone on the corridor, and surely Miss Wade and the children would be well in bed by now. Once she got into the nursery, half her troubles would be over. She could easily slip into the brush room and unless Miss Wade was in the sitting-room instead of her bedroom, chances of anyone hearing her were small. All she had to do then was press the knob, go down the secret stairs to the drawing-room, and wait until the guests had gone to bed.

She decided to wait a little longer, until Nellie was asleep and all the other servants had gone to bed. As she lay awake, staring into the darkness, she couldn't help wishing she had her own watch with its illuminated dial. How very unhandy everything was in those days!

As she was afraid to bring a candle with her, she could only hope that the lights would still be on. But she took the matches from the bedroom, with a silent prayer that Nellie wouldn't wake up and want to light her candle. 'Nothing much she can do about it, if she does!' she thought in grim amusement.

Luck was with her and she successfully negotiated the servants' corridor, the back stairs and the nursery corridor. Gently turning the handle she slipped into the nursery and then the brush room. Everything was as silent as the grave. Everyone must be asleep. She pressed the knob and the panel opened with the familiar click. Then, lighting her candle, she went down the secret stairs.

As she noiselessly pushed the panel at the foot of the stairs, she could hear voices. So the guests had *not* gone to bed yet. Well, all she had to do was wait. Surely Lady Tyrconnell would, in her tinkling voice, order them all off to bed shortly.

But as she listened, she became aware that there were no female voices to be heard. They had obviously gone to bed and left the men behind. It soon became apparent that they were having a heated argument, and her heart sank. Maybe they would be there until the small hours. Grimly she decided she would stay, no matter how late it was.

'My dear Tyrconnell,' one was saying. Lucy could just see him — a tall man with reddish hair. 'You must see that this spirit of unrest is being fomented. Especially by the local clergy. Father McFadden is simply inflaming the people with all this talk of withholding rents. I believe he actually preaches it from the pulpit.'

'Pity his superiors don't take him in hand,' growled a small fat man. That must be Fitzgerald; Lucy couldn't suppress a giggle when she remembered Nellie's description of him — 'Too fat to get out of his own way.' 'The Pope ... Cardinal

Manning . . . all the bishops are against the political involvement of the clergy. The country is getting out of control. Not a day goes by without people who have taken evicted land being beaten up and process servers being stoned. Why I'm told that in certain parts, writs have to be sent by post. It's no longer safe to serve them in person.'

'But nobody can deny that the people are in a bad way.' Lucy recognised the voice of Lord Tyrconnell. 'The last two years have been hard. Dry springs. Summer droughts. Cattle and butter prices down. What do you think, Gordon?'

'I can support that. My agent tells me he's getting less than half the prices he got for cattle two years ago.'

'We can only be patient and wait for better times. We are not suffering as our tenants are.'

'Patient? We're all standing meekly by while our whole way of life is being undermined. What about that disgraceful land act of Gladstone's?' That was the ginger-haired man.

'Fair rent, fixity of tenure, freedom of sale? Can we really quarrel with that, Rossmartin? Surely that was a just measure. And has it made much difference to us? I'm told that at most it amounts to a ten per cent reduction in income.'

'And if we can't afford that ten per cent?' Fitzgerald's voice was even more heated. 'Does anyone ask what *our* circumstances are? Look at the Kingston estate! Practically beggared!'

'Fitzgerald, you know that act was a necessity. Even Parliament realised that. You don't think the members would have passed it except for all the unrest in Ireland.'

'We can thank the Land League for all that. Good thing they suppressed it in '81.'

'And what have we got in its place? The Irish National League. Almost as many members and twice the influence. And they're no longer concerned with fair rents and tenure — they want the whole country.'

'If only they'd hurry up,' fretted Lucy. 'Don't they know they're not going to solve anything!'

'Parnell is behind it all. He's dropped the land issue, wants to break free of England.'

'Fellow should be horsewhipped. He's nothing but a renegade. A disgrace to his class and his religion.'

'Mother was American — that explains a lot. Half-baked ideas of equality.'

'Bad enough to have that goat Gladstone hand in glove with him — did you read his speech on Home Rule at Midlothian? But what are the Conservatives playing at? Expected more of old Salisbury. Couldn't believe he'd let the Coercion Act lapse.'

'Pressure, I suspect. He wants the support of Parnell and his party.'

'So we're being held to ransom by a buccaneer like that. Whatever way we vote, Home Rule is on the agenda.'

'But why shouldn't Ireland have a say in her own affairs? Are we against that?'

'My dear Tyrconnell, what are you saying? Home Rule would be the death knell of the landlord class in Ireland.'

'But all that's suggested, Rossmartin, is a limited form of self-government, something like Colonial status. Ireland would remain within the Empire. At present we're pawns in the British game. Why do you think prices are so depressed? It's because of Free Trade. The English can unload all their goods here. We're powerless to fight them. We have no voice. All decisions are made in London.'

'But will Home Rule satisfy Parnell? Mark my words: Home Rule today. Complete separation tomorrow.'

'And what's the alternative? Coercion today. Rebellion tomorrow. And eventually a separate state?'

'We're pawns, all right,' said Fitzgerald bitterly, 'in the struggle between Conservatives and Liberals. With this election coming up, who knows what the end result will be.'

'I understand Parnell is already come to Avondale. For the shooting.' Rossmartin's voice dropped to a whisper but Lucy,

ears strained, heard, 'I understand Captain O'Shea refused an invitation there.'

'Of course,' she thought. 'It's the 1885 election!'

'Never mind O'Shea,' snapped Fitzgerald. 'Parnell is here to cause trouble. He started his campaign in Arklow and followed it up with more electioneering at the Lord Mayor's banquet in Dublin.'

'Why doesn't he stay at home and look after his own affairs? Then he wouldn't have to be getting up public subscriptions to pay off his mortgage. That was a nice kettle of fish!'

'Oh, that's not quite fair,' came the drawling voice of Lord Gordon. '*He* didn't get up the subscription . . . I wish somebody would come along to me . . . with an offer of £40,000 . . .'

There was laughter, and then came the voice of Lord Tyrconnell, 'Now, gentlemen, I really think it is time we retired . . . we have an early start in the morning. Let's leave the affairs of the nation for the night. Nothing we can say or do here will alter anything.'

There was a general movement and the sound of chairs being pushed back.

Lord Gordon's voice sounded again. 'Must tell you the damndest story I heard of Parnell. There was, as you know, a public presentation of that famous cheque. In Morrison's Hotel in Dublin. Everyone there — speeches at the ready — supper waiting to be served — Lord Mayor in chains of office. In comes Parnell and says, before the poor man can get a word out, "I believe you have a cheque for me." Stunned Mayor produces it, and starts into his speech once again, whereupon Parnell asks, "Is it made payable to order and crossed?" On being told it is, he takes the cheque, puts it into his waistcoat pocket and departs.'

His last words drifted back to Lucy.

'As Sexton whispered to Tim Healy, "A labourer would acknowledge the loan of a penknife more gratefully . . ."'

'Well, that's not quite my reading of it. It must have been a humiliating experience for him . . .'

'You talk as if you admired him. Really, Tyrconnell . . .'

As the voices finally faded, Lucy thought, 'Thank goodness. They've actually gone. Strong, silent men! Don't they ever stop talking?'

Just as she was about to adjust the panel so that she could squeeze into the room, a sound froze her in her tracks. Hastily she pressed the panel back into position, leaving just the barest slit.

Winters and McGinley had come into the drawing-room. Of course! They would have to check the lights and the fire. It seemed ages before they left but finally she could hear the doors closing. Opening the panel, she crept out, shielding her candle with her hand in case any tell-tale flicker might be seen. She hastened over to the bureau and opened the drawer with nervous hands.

It was empty. There was no little box. No ring. Lady Tyrconnell must have taken it upstairs with her!

Back in bed, Lucy was too agitated to sleep. If only she could convince Robert she came from the twentieth century. Then he would help her to get the ring.

A sudden idea came to her and her brain began to race. A mental image of her bedroom floated through her mind. She could hear her father talking and see the book, *Simple Science*, sitting on the shelf. 'Surely I can remember something,' she thought. 'I *did* read bits of it. What was that experiment about electricity? The one that David and I did? That would prove to Robert that I'm not talking off the top of my head. I'll think about it tomorrow — I'm sure I can remember it . . . it was really quite simple . . .'

She fell into an exhausted sleep, and dreamt about the ruby ring. She had it in her hand but the shadowy figure of the sallow faced man was chasing her. Then she fell and the man was shaking her, trying to take the ring away. She screamed and woke suddenly.

Nellie was shaking her, saying, 'It's all right, Lucy, you were having a bad dream. But you must hurry now. It's time to get up . . . Now, where are those matches . . .?'

## 10   The Experiment

That morning all was activity again. When she had set the fires and cleaned the nursery, Lucy helped Minnie to bring up the hot water cans. In the kitchen preparations for the shooting party were going ahead. Mrs O'Shea was packing pies and cold meats into great hampers and casseroles in earthenware jars were being put into hay-boxes. 'Keeps the food hot for hours,' explained Florrie.

'Do the ladies go shooting too?' asked Lucy as she and Nellie ate their bread and butter.

'Not all of them. Lady Rossmartin does. She's a great shot, I hear. The other ladies join the guns for lunch.'

'A picnic?'

'I'd hardly call it a picnic,' grinned Nellie. 'They have tablecloths and tables and glasses and wine and everything. And Winters and McGinley to serve them.'

'What happens if it's raining?'

'They stay at home! Or they might arrange lunch at one of the outlying barns.'

'They take an awful lot of food with them, don't they?'

'Not really. In addition to the house party, there will be some other gentlemen from round about. Then there are the beaters and the staff . . .'

'Beaters?'

'You've never been to a shoot, have you?'

'No. I suppose they just go out to the fields and shoot anything they see.'

'Bless you, no. They have a lot of young fellows — they're the beaters. They form a line and march forward, beating the undergrowth as they go. The birds rise and then the shooters, who are told where to stand, fire at them.'

'The birds don't have much chance, do they?'

'Not much. But they don't have much time to think about it! It's all over in a flash. Then the gun-dogs retrieve them and at the end of the day they're brought in here ... and Maggie and I spend our time plucking the feathers.'

'... I know what you're going to say — that they'll die anyway — but it seems cruel.'

'Lucy, the breakfast trays.' Bella Jane broke in on their conversation, and Lucy hurried off. Elizabeth seemed in a particularly bad humour and Lucy wondered if she was still upset about not being allowed to keep the ring.

'I think we'll forego lessons this morning,' Miss Wade was saying when Lucy returned later, having left the trays back to the kitchen. 'We're expecting a visitor and Lady Tyrconnell wants you to look your prettiest, Elizabeth.'

Elizabeth said nothing. She rose and went into her room. Miss Wade sighed and said, 'I want to see Mrs Morris this morning about changing the summer curtains. Lucy, you can help Elizabeth to dress.'

'And get my head chopped off!' thought Lucy, concluding that Miss Wade had had enough of Elizabeth for one morning.

'Robert,' said Miss Wade as she was departing, 'get out the magic lantern. It may amuse Frederick.'

'A magic lantern. What's that?' wondered Lucy.

Robert returned to the table with a black box, the sides of which were decorated with scrolls of brasswork. Taking a large square of white material, he placed it against the wall, securing it with straight pins from the sewing-box.

'Like to see it? I'll just light the candle and then we're ready.'

Taking the box of matches from the mantelpiece, he lifted a lid at the back and lit the candle within. Then from another box, he withdrew a square slide and slowly drew it across the lens of the magic lantern. As Lucy looked at the white screen, the garishly painted figure of ghouls and demons were projected on to the screen.

'What do you think of my magic lantern, Lucy?'

Lucy chuckled. 'It's primitive TV,' she told him.

'TV? What a peculiar word. What does it mean?'

Lucy could have clapped! This was her chance to prove to Robert that she came from another age.

'TV is really short for television, and we watch it quite a lot in my time. Figures appear on a screen rather like your lantern.'

'Does your father get the slides and work it for you?' asked Robert, puzzled.

'No, no. We just have to plug it in and switch it on. It's worked by electricity. The electric current passes through the plug and the wire and switches on the set. As well as seeing pictures, we can hear the people talk.'

'What does this TV look like?'

'It's really just a large box, with glass in front, and it has a screen which is called a tube and lots of wires inside. I'm not much good explaining how it works but I *can* tell you about electricity.' She now had the experiment that David and she tried firmly fixed in her mind.

'I want to show you something. But first I need a glass, a woollen cloth, a little piece of paper, fairly heavy, a scissors and a cork.'

'I have a drinking glass in my room ...'

'Good ... there's sure to be a bit of woollen cloth in the brush room. There's plenty of paper and I'll borrow the scissors from the work box here. Now all I need is a cork.'

She didn't fancy going down to the kitchen for one, so she darted into Miss Wade's room. Sure enough, the governess had a bottle of cordial on her bedside table. 'I'm sure she won't mind if I borrow the cork for a few moments,' thought Lucy, hoping there would be no interruptions until she had successfully completed the experiment.

Robert had put his glass on the table, and Lucy made sure that it was perfectly dry. Then she cut a cross from the paper which she pointed at one end.

'I forgot; I need a needle as well,' and she took one from the sewing-box. She pushed the needle into the cork and skewered the paper cross to it. Then she placed the glass over the cork and the needle with the cross.

Taking the woollen cloth, she explained, 'By rubbing the glass with this cloth, I will charge the glass with electricity,' and as she slowly began to rub a part of the glass she said, 'Watch the pointed end of the paper ...'

She held her breath, afraid that it would not work. For a moment she thought she saw the cross quiver ... but nothing happened. Robert looked at her curiously.

'It's supposed to work,' said Lucy angrily. 'The object of the exercise is to create an electric charge so that the pointed end of the cross turns to face the part I've rubbed. By rubbing the glass all round, you can make the cross revolve. It works. I *know* it works. I've done it before. Maybe the glass isn't

dry enough. David and I warmed it in the oven before. That's it. We'll try again.'

When she turned to look at Robert, he was laughing.

'Oh, Lucy, I didn't have the heart to tell you before. I know a little about electricity — it was the TV I was interested in.'

'How can you know about electricity?' asked Lucy miserably.

'We have had it installed in our house in London. It's also in the House of Commons, and there are quite a few electric inventions of all kinds around — hot-plates, for instance, and kettles. We can't use them here of course.'

'So much for *Simple Science*,' thought Lucy savagely, wishing she had the little book so that she could kick it into outer space. Aloud she said, 'Surely the fact that I know about electricity and could tell you about inventions of the future proves that I don't belong to this age.'

'I do believe you, Lucy,' said Robert slowly.

'Then you'll help me to get the ring back.'

'I'll try.'

Lucy's heart sank. He had not been convinced. He really didn't believe her. And he certainly wasn't going to cross that dragon of a mother of his to help a nursery-maid.

'I think you should go in to Elizabeth,' said Robert unhappily. 'Miss Wade will expect her to be dressed for going out when she comes back.'

Before Lucy had time to do anything, the door opened and Miss Wade came in, accompanied by a tall boy dressed for riding.

'Hello, Robert,' he said, then looking around, 'Where's Miss Elizabeth?'

'Yes, where is Elizabeth?' Miss Wade looked sternly at Lucy.

'She ... she said she would get ready herself,' said Robert and Lucy sighed with relief. 'Hello, Frederick, would you like to see my magic lantern?'

'Later,' said Frederick smiling. 'I hoped we would all go

out riding. It's such a beautiful sunny morning.'

Miss Wade went in to fetch Elizabeth, who came out a little later. She had not changed from her dark blue dress, which looked all rumpled as if she had been lying on it.

'We're going riding, Miss Elizabeth,' said Frederick. 'At least Robert and I are. I hoped you would come with us.'

'No, I don't think so.' Elizabeth's voice was edgy. 'I've really more to do with my time.'

'Elizabeth!' Miss Wade sounded shocked. She seemed about to order Elizabeth to get into her riding-clothes. Then she evidently thought better of it. 'Elizabeth has not been very well lately,' she explained to Frederick. 'Perhaps it would be better if she went to bed for the day.'

Elizabeth flounced back into her room and Frederick, looking crestfallen, went off with Robert. Miss Wade accompanied them, saying she would bring them down to the stables.

Lucy tip-toed into Elizabeth's room. She was lying on her bed, face down on her pillow, her shoulders heaving with sobs. 'Spoilt creature,' thought Lucy. She felt like leaving her to her own devices but something of the misery that she had seen in her face made her pause. She suddenly remembered her father saying — how long ago that had been? — 'No matter how bad things are for you, there's always someone worse off.' Going up to the bed, she looked down at Elizabeth and said very gently, 'Is there anything wrong? Can I help?'

Elizabeth was so surprised that she turned over and sat up. 'You! A servant-maid! What can *you* do to help me?'

'Not much,' returned Lucy, trying to sound cheerful. 'But my father used to say that if you talk things over, somehow they don't seem so bad.'

'Is your father dead?' asked Elizabeth, a note of sympathy creeping into her voice.

'As good as,' said Lucy, trying not to think of home. 'I'm a long way from him and I wonder will I ever see him again.'

'Oh, Lucy,' cried Elizabeth, 'I'm so miserable. I don't know

what to do. And I can't ask anyone for advice.'

'Would you like to tell me about it?' asked Lucy.

'Sit down — on the bed — and I'll try.' Twisting her lace-edged handkerchief around her fingers, Elizabeth went on, 'It's just that Mamma wants me to marry Frederick. He's the son of the Earl of Gordon and that would mean I'd be a Countess one day. Mamma is a Viscountess and she's determined that I should marry well.'

It sounded all so strange to Lucy that she wondered if she was hearing Elizabeth aright.

'You mean that at your age ...'

'Twelve,' said Elizabeth. 'This week-end.'

'... your mother is planning your marriage. Aren't you a little young?'

'Not now ... in a few years' time. You see, Frederick is the most eligible catch, as Mamma puts it, in the whole neighbourhood ... and she's set her heart on him. Oh, I know it's not immediate. I'll come out when I'm sixteen and I'll have a season first in Dublin and then in London. Mamma says that I'll be disgraced if I don't get engaged in my first season. Frederick would be doing the seasons too, so she's trying to ensure he won't look any further than me ...'

'What will happen if you don't get engaged in your first season ... or if Frederick falls in love with someone else?'

Lucy was still trying to come to terms with the fact that one's life might be finished at sixteen.

'Oh, if you're a failure after your first season, they pack you off to India.'

'India?'

'So many army people are out there. Usually younger sons and so on. And there are very few girls around. So nearly all the girls who go out come back engaged.'

'And if you didn't?'

'I would just have to live on here, being somebody's aunt. When we visited Coole Hall last year, there were these three sisters who hadn't married. They were just there on suffrance. Nobodies. Living on charity. I don't want that to happen to me.'

Lucy thought to herself in some amusement, 'Well, you're certainly not helping yourself by scaring away prospective suitors,' but she didn't say it aloud. Instead she asked, 'Do you like Frederick?'

'Oh, he's all right ... for a boy. Always talking about his dog and his horse ...'

'Well, you like Sparkle too, don't you?'

'That's true. And he *is* nice and we have a lot to talk about whenever we meet. And he gets on well with Robert. And his place — Glenrea Castle — is very near so I would still see a lot of Robert. I really like Robert a lot, though you mightn't think it.'

'You could have fooled me,' thought Lucy.

'And now I've made a mess of everything,' said Elizabeth, bursting into tears again. 'It's just that Mamma expects so much of me. She'll be asking me how we got on today, and what Frederick said, and what I said. And if I ever say or do anything of which she doesn't approve, she gets so cold and reproving. Oh, Lucy, it's just that I hate being *pushed* at Frederick. Why can't they leave us alone?'

'What does your father think?'

'Papa? He likes Frederick and I know he'd like the marriage. But he always says, when Mamma talks about these things, that I must make up my own mind. Oh, Lucy, I'm so miserable. I just don't know what to do.'

'And I thought *I* had problems,' groaned Lucy silently. She stood up and said briskly, 'Well, here's what you must do.'

Elizabeth looked up in amazement, surprised at the authority in Lucy's voice. 'Dry your eyes and I'll splash some cold water on them so that no one will know you have been crying. Now, where are your riding things . . .'

'I can't go now . . . Frederick will think it so odd . . . besides they'll be gone by now . . .'

'No, they won't — they were going to look at the pups first.' Lucy ran to the window of Robert's bedroom which looked out over the stable courtyard. Opening it, she leaned out and shouted, 'Robert . . . Master Robert . . .' She was rewarded by the sight of Robert who appeared from one of the stables. 'Wait . . . Miss Elizabeth will be down in a few minutes.'

'Great!' said Frederick, who had joined Robert.

'Hurry,' said Lucy, helping Elizabeth into her dark-green riding-habit. She tied back her fair hair, helped her to find her riding-cap and her gloves and sent her off.

'Don't explain anything. Just say you couldn't find your habit or you had a nose-bleed. Frederick isn't going to cross-examine you!'

Watching from the window, she saw Elizabeth join the others and, laughing and talking together, they took their ponies from the stables and set off through the courtyard.

'And that,' said Lucy ruefully as she closed the window,

'is that. I wish I had someone to help *me* solve my problems.'

When she went back into the sitting-room Miss Wade had returned. 'I hope, Lucy,' she said, 'that that wasn't you who yelled out of the window at Master Robert.' As Lucy gave a guilty flush, she continued, smiling, 'Still you got Elizabeth to join them and that is something. Now, it's almost time for lunch. As the children are not here, I'll go downstairs today.'

Preparations for that evening's dinner were just as hectic as on the day before, and Lucy slaved away all afternoon, fetching and carrying, chopping and shredding, until she thought she could stand it no longer. The shooting party returned about three o'clock and then there was the bustle of tea, and later the bringing up of the hot water to the bedrooms. Lucy was dying to know how Elizabeth had got on with Frederick but as Miss Wade was there when she took up the supper trays, she was unable to speak to her. Elizabeth, however, flashed her a grateful smile, so Lucy concluded that things had gone off well.

As Lucy worked with Nellie loading up the lift, her mind was busily working out a plan of campaign. She must go to Lady Tyrconnell's room and get the ring — there was no other course of action. Robert was not prepared to help her and in her heart she could not blame him. Now she was on her own.

Surely there must be some time when Lady Tyrconnell's room was empty. She kept her eyes and ears open over the next few days and finally decided that the best time would be in the evening. When the ladies had gone down to dinner, Spencer would go to supper in The Room. Dinner in the dining-room lasted about two hours or more, and in The Room, so Bella Jane told her, the upper servants, except for Winters, McGinley and Patrick of course, tended to relax and take longer over their supper, secure in the knowledge that nobody would want them until it was time to go to bed. But where would the ring be? It was important to find out, as she intended to spend as little time as possible in the bedroom.

One evening, when she was leaving up the water, she positioned herself so that she got a good look into the room when Spencer opened the door. The sour-faced lady's-maid took the cans from her, almost pushing her back. But the quick glance that Lucy had taken showed that to the left of the big four-poster bed was the fireplace, and against the wall a small table and chair. No, the ring would surely be kept in the dressing-table or Lady Tyrconnell's jewel case.

That evening, when the dinner-gong sounded, she said urgently to Nellie as they were loading the dishes into the lift, 'Nellie — could you cover for me for a little while?'

Nellie looked at her doubtfully. 'You're not up to anything you shouldn't be,' she whispered.

'No, of course not. I just need a few minutes to myself. If anyone asks you anything, say I felt faint and went to get a drink of water.'

She slipped up the back stairs and along the corridor until she came to Lady Tyrconnell's bedroom, the centre one on the landing. Then, hearing someone coming up the stairs, she shrank back into the shadow of the huge potted palm on the landing. The someone was Spencer and she was carrying a tray. She must be working on clothes for Lady Tyrconnell and decided to have her supper in the bedroom.

Cursing her luck, Lucy skipped down and rejoined Nellie. 'All clear,' said the latter cheerfully. 'Now that I've covered for you, what are you going to do for me?

'You'll be amazed when you find out.' replied Lucy. Strangely, in spite of her failure to get into Lady Tyrconnell's room, she felt her spirits rising. It was only a question of time before she did. She just had to keep her wits about her and seize the first opportunity. 'If at first you don't succeed, try and try again,' she sang as they darted to and fro with dishes and platters and casseroles.

When they went to bed that night, Nellie, usually so cheerful, seemed very preoccupied. When Lucy was just about to drop into a tired sleep, she thought she heard a sob. Sitting up, she asked what was wrong.

'Oh, Lucy, I do try. You see how I do. But sometimes it just comes over me. Tonight when they were talking at supper about Christmas and what they would do if they got a day off, I thought of home. We used to have Christmas. Nothing very much — we couldn't afford it. But sometimes we would have a bit of mutton and Ma once baked a cake with raisins in it. And we walked to Mass. We were all together then.'

'Oh, Nellie, I am sorry,' Lucy was contrite. Engrossed in her own problems she had forgotten all about Nellie. And yet their situations were so similar. Both were separated from their families, though Lucy felt she had a chance of returning to hers. An exciting thought suddenly struck her. 'Nellie, surely your Aunt Annie knew where your father and mother were going to?'

'Aye, they were going to me Uncle John in New York,' said Nellie forlornly.

'If only we had an address we could contact them. Write to them, I mean. If only you had a letter from them.'

'There was no letter, Lucy. The only thing I have is an old piece of paper that me aunt gave me before she died. I think she was trying to tell me something, but her talking had gone so funny before that that I didn't know what she was saying. It seemed to content her when I took the piece of paper. I kept it with me ever since. Not that I can make anything of it. It's funny joined-up writing . . .'

'Oh, Nellie,' Lucy jumped out of bed and threw her arms around her. 'You can't read. Is that it?'

'It is. I'm ashamed but that's how it is. But I can write me name in grand big letters.'

'That's great!' Lucy was unable to keep the excitement from her voice as she asked, 'Could I see this piece of paper?'

'Surely you can.' Getting out of bed, Nellie rummaged around in the top drawer of the rickety chest and took out a folded piece of paper. Lucy smoothed out the paper, glad that there weren't too many folds, and read out, 'Mister John Magee'.

Clutching her by the arm Nellie said in a choking voice, 'That's me uncle!' Lucy smiled and continued:

c/o Mister Charles Linderman
18 Rose Street
New York, America

'Me Uncle John was to help me father get a job ... and now I know where he lives. Maybe he'll know where to find me family. To think I was carrying this round for so long and never knew what it was.' Nellie's voice was sad but she added in a determined tone, 'Somehow I'm going to have to learn to read and write proper ... Lucy, how come you can read so well?'

Lucy hesitated and said, 'That's a long story, Nellie, and it doesn't matter at the moment. What we must do now is get a letter off to America and see if we can find your people.'

'How much would that cost?' asked Nellie.

'I don't know ... but I have a plan. Leave it all to me.'

She had already decided she would ask Robert. Surely he would help. But she didn't tell Nellie. It would be too dreadful if nothing came of it. Best not say anything and let the outcome be a surprise.

'I can't promise anything, Nellie,' she said, 'so just say your prayers and hope for the best ... now, you're always telling me to go to sleep ... this time, I'm telling you.'

Lucy had a chance to talk to Robert the very next day as Elizabeth and Frederick, accompanied by Miss Wade, went for a walk. Robert decided to stay behind.

'Lucy,' he began, 'I've been thinking a lot of what you said

— about coming from another age. The electricity didn't really prove it. Can you tell me something that is about to happen ... that you already know about? Am I making myself clear?'

Lucy could have kicked herself. 'But of course! How absolutely stupid not to have thought of that. What sort of thing do you want to know?' praying fervently it would not be something she knew nothing about.

'The election we've just had. What happened?'

'The 1885 election?'

'Yes. There's all this talk — they go on about it interminably — about the Liberals and the Conservatives and Parnell. And about Home Rule and Gladstone?'

'Thank heavens for Parnell,' thought Lucy. 'Robert,' she said solemnly, 'Parnell got 86 seats ... That was the exact difference between the Liberals and Conservatives so the Irish party held the balance of power.'

'Are you sure, Lucy? Papa and the others were so sure the Conservatives would win ... they'll be furious. And what happened after that?'

'My memory is a big vague,' said Lucy. 'I have a feeling that the Conservatives wouldn't support Home Rule and that there was another election later and Gladstone tried to introduce it and failed. I know I should know more but I've forgotten.'

'Lucy,' said Robert severely, 'you're making all this up, aren't you?'

Lucy laughed. 'Well, you'll soon find out, won't you? The results will be announced any day now. Just remember — Parnell 86 seats — now I couldn't have made that up unless it was true. And the beauty is you'll soon find out.'

'All we can do is wait,' decided Robert soberly. 'And if what you've told me is right, I'll help you to get the ring.'

Lucy was feeling in exuberant mood. Surely, any day now, all her troubles would be at an end.

'And for my next trick, Robert,' she said gleefully, 'I propose to show you how to get down to the drawing-room without going through the main house.'

'Lucy, that's impossible,' cried Robert. 'You surely don't mean to climb out through the window.'

'And float down to the ground? No! I have a much simpler way. Take the matches and come with me.'

Robert followed her into the brush room. She lit the candle, said in a chanting voice 'Abracadabra' and pressed the knob. There was a click and the panel swung open.

'A secret staircase,' gasped Robert. 'It was there all the time and nobody knew about it.'

Lucy nodded. 'I found it by accident. Now, go down very carefully, and at the foot of the stairs you'll find a panel facing you. Press it and it will swing inward. By pushing, you can increase the gap so that you can get into the room.'

'Lucy, how do you know?'

'I tried it . . . now, go down and try it too. But don't appear in the drawing-room if there's anyone there!'

Robert came back, a few minutes later, his face flushed with excitement. 'How wonderful! I must tell Elizabeth. We'll be able to play all kinds of games here.'

'And now, I want you to do me a favour, Robert?' said Lucy as they went back to the schoolroom. 'No, not the ring. That can wait.'

She sat down at the table facing him and told him the story of Nellie, the eviction, her illness, the family going to America, and her aunt's death.

'What a tragedy,' said Robert. 'How can I help?'

'We have the address to which her family went. If we can write them a letter, maybe they'll get in touch with her again.'

'Of course.'

Taking a piece of paper, Lucy wrote a short letter telling the family that Nellie was at Langley Castle in Donegal and could be contacted care of Master Robert Tyrconnell. 'It's best that they address the letter to you — you will get it, won't you?'

'Of course. McGinley collects the post and he'll make sure I get it.'

'Now the only problem is how to get the letter out. I've no money. Have you?'

'Not much,' Robert turned out his pockets which held marbles, chestnuts and an old coin. 'Don't worry, I'll ring for McGinley.' When the footman came in, Robert said. 'McGinley, I have a letter to go to America. Make sure it gets the next post.'

'Certainly, Master Robert,' said McGinley.

'And don't let anyone else handle it. You're to take it to the post yourself and make sure it gets off safely.'

'Cross my heart,' vowed McGinley, taking the letter and departing, with the barest twinkle of a wink at Lucy.

'Such a nice man,' said Robert. 'I believe he's learning Irish. He tells me Florrie and Maggie are fluent speakers.'

'How on earth did you know that?' asked Lucy.

'A little bird told me.' Robert was not to be drawn. 'And he himself has taught me a few words:

*Tir gan teanga*
*Tir gan anam.*

Do you know what that means?'

'I do indeed,' replied Lucy:

A country without a tongue
Is a country without a soul . . .

Goodness, look at the time. Mrs O'Shea will want my head on a plate.'

'Sorry,' she explained when she got down to the kitchen, 'I had to stay with Master Robert.'

'Just sitting around, I'll be bound. He's too big now for a nurse-maid. Here, you'll have to help out in the laundry. There's a mountain of work to be done, and that wretched extra girl never turned in.'

After dinner, Lucy went to the laundry, which was a low-ceilinged room with roughly plastered walls. It was quite warm as there was a fire burning and she could see two large copper urns sitting on the steel plate which covered the fire; behind them was a large boiler.

As she hesitated, a girl came through from another room and introduced herself as Mary Kate — Lucy remembered having seen her that first morning they went to Mass.

'Becky and me have some of the soiled articles steeping since early this morning so they should be ready for washing now.'

Bending over one of the tubs, which was wide on top and narrow at the base, she pulled a plug and let the water drain away. Then she refilled it with clean water. Handing Lucy a bar of yellow soap she said, 'Rub the clothes and things against each other — saves the hands.'

As Lucy was scrubbing, thinking wistfully of the washing machine at home, Becky came through from the other room, which Mary Kate told her was the ironing and drying room. 'We wash the clothes twice, then they are boiled, then rinsed, then put through the mangle ...'

Lucy had been wondering what the strange-looking objects were. Each looked like two giant rolling pins, with black iron handles. Now she knew that they were mangles for wringing out excess water.

The afternoon passed slowly and she smiled in welcome relief when Nellie came in to fetch her to bring up the nursery trays.

'I think the laundry is even worse than the kitchen,' she said to Nellie as they went along to the kitchen.

'Well, we've had a terrible day of it. I've been plucking grouse all day and there's that much yet to do that I doubt we'll ever get finished.'

In spite of her resolution not to say anything to Nellie, Lucy couldn't resist telling her about the letter. At the back of her mind was the thought that if she were to get the ring within the next few days and get back home, Nellie would know nothing of the letter. At least now she could ask McGinley.

Laundry work continued after tea and as Lucy slaved away, she wondered if Mrs O'Shea would soon be yelling for her to take up the hot water or help Nellie. But strangely she didn't. Neither did Nellie, and Lucy thought she might be trying to give her a rest. So when they finished in the laundry, she didn't go back to the kitchen. She hung about the passages leading to the courtyard and then went out into the yard. It was a still frosty night with thousands of stars in the sky — Lucy could never remember seeing so many before. 'Probably all the pollution we get,' she thought. The few leaves still left on the trees rustled together and the bare branches were sharply etched against the sky. A pale crescent moon was beginning to rise over a clump of oak-trees.

The game larder was full of birds suspended by the necks — more plucking for Nellie in the morning.

At long last she heard the loud boom of the dinner-gong. Maybe tonight her plan to get the ring from Lady Tyrconnell's room would work. Then she wouldn't have to wait until Robert finally believed her story. She smiled as she thought of how surprised he would be to find the ring gone, her gone ... and Parnell with his 86 seats! Then she decided that even if she got the ring she would definitely stay on to say good-bye to Robert and to Elizabeth, who had been very nice to her ever since that morning in the schoolroom ....

Heart in mouth, Lucy slipped up the back stairs and along the corridor until she came to Lady Tyrconnell's bedroom door. She turned the knob and slid into the room. A tall oil lamp stood on a table and the shadow of the four-poster bed danced against the walls in the flickering firelight. A door opened off the main bedroom and Lucy thought that this must be Lady Tyrconnell's dressing-room. Peeping inside, she saw a dressing-table against the wall, a dark heavy piece of furniture with many drawers. By the light cast by an ornate lamp standing on a small round table, she could see a black leather box on the table, surrounded by perfume bottles. That must be her jewel-case.

She was about to step forward and open it, when she heard the sound of voices outside the room. She stood rooted to the spot and listened.

The two voices belonged to Mrs Morris and Spencer, who had evidently met on the stairs.

'Are you not coming down for supper?' asked the housekeeper in a concerned tone of voice. Lucy held her breath.

'No. Her Ladyship was particularly hard to please when dressing for dinner, so I have a lot of costumes to put away. And indeed renovate some that she found fault with. I will wait here until she comes up after dinner and I can get something later.'

'I'll send up a tray if you like,' said Mrs Morris, lingering.

'No, I wouldn't dream of putting anyone to that trouble,' Spencer said quickly, almost, thought Lucy, as if she were trying to get rid of the housekeeper.

'Well, I hope you don't have to wait up too late.'

'I'll snatch forty winks,' said Spencer yawning, 'in between my work. You know what it's like when there are guests.'

Lucy had returned to the bedroom and was now looking wildly around for a place to hide. Her gaze came to rest on a tall painted screen which stood just behind the bedroom door, and she dived behind it.

'How odd!' said Spencer, as she went into the room. 'I thought I had closed the door when I went down.'

'Well, it seems you didn't,' said Mrs Morris genially. 'Really, Spencer, you don't seem to have your mind on your work these days!'

'Her ladyship has no complaints,' said Spencer tartly, as with a curt good-night she closed the door.

Lucy stood still as a statue as Spencer, her dress swishing, seemed to come very close to the screen. There was no chance of looking for the ring tonight. Her main worry now was the fear of being discovered. She would have to bide her time until Spencer's back was turned and slip out. But how would she know when? She dared not risk a look around the screen.

Just as she had decided to make a dash for it, there was a very gentle rap at the door. Then another rap. Then someone sidled into the room.

'Patrick! What are you doing here?' Spencer sounded both alarmed and angry.

'I had to chance it,' Patrick's voice was low and urgent. 'Why don't we take it now and run for it?'

'You can't steal it from her Ladyship's room. She knows she's left it here in her jewel-box.'

'Anyone could have taken it from here,' he whined.

'I'm the only person with access to this room. Suspicion would fall on me straightway.'

'Not on you. Honest Spencer! She already thinks that that little girl Lucy is after the ring. She'll suspect her.'

'Patrick, I can't. Not now. You'll have to leave it to me

to choose the right moment.'

'I'm tired hanging around. I don't like being ordered around all the time. If you love me like you say you do, you'd take the ring now.'

'What a crew,' thought Lucy, petrified not only with fear but now with anger.

'Patrick.' Spencer's voice was chill. 'Get downstairs at once, or Winters will notice you're missing. I had a hard enough time getting him to take you back after your last flight.'

'I'll go ... but I'm warning you. I'm not going to wait ...'

'Meet me tomorrow in the walled garden and we'll plan everything. Twelve o'clock. Now go!'

He opened the door and Lucy could hear his footsteps crossing the door saddle. Luckily, he left it ajar. Lucy peeped round the screen very cautiously. Spencer hadn't noticed the open door and she was taking a dress from the wardrobe. Lucy crept out from behind the screen and slipped through the door.

She raced down the stairs to the servants' hall. What was she to do? She would have to tell Robert and they would have to go along to the garden tomorrow and hear what the pair were planning. But it was only a question of time before they stole the ring ... and blamed her. She would be sent away in disgrace and never get home.

## 11　Plots

Next morning, when she brought up the breakfast trays, she was in for rather a shock.

'You can take that one down again,' said Miss Wade apologetically. 'I forgot to tell the kitchen. Elizabeth and Robert are away to visit Frederick. As it's a long ride, they and Fielding left a short while ago.'

So Robert wouldn't be with her — to hear the plotting of the schemers. She would have to do it on her own. The only question now was, 'How would she manage to slip away?'

In the end it turned out to be surprisingly easy. She had been sent down to the kitchen for the morning and soon after she arrived there, McDyer came in with his vegetables. Mrs. O'Shea checked them over. 'Onions, celery, broccoli, leeks, lamb's lettuce . . . where's the Savoy cabbage?'

'Never ordered it!' McDyer shook a gnarled finger at her.

'Don't know what's coming over me these days. I'll be forgetting my own name next. I must have that cabbage for my boiled bacon. Can you get it sent up? Not you. Is there anyone down there?'

'No, the boys are away at the shoot. Where's Patrick?'

'Nowhere in sight. Lying around somewhere, no doubt, like a heap of last year's turf. Useless fellow . . . Here, what about you, Lucy? Go down with McDyer and bring back the cabbage. Three good heads, mind you. Get your cloak, girl.

As she left the kitchen, Lucy looked at the clock. It was a quarter past ten. The cabbages weren't wanted until later in the day. She would have enough time to go to the gardens with McDyer and slip into the walled garden on the way back.

As they went through the yard, they were joined by a variety of dogs and McDyer told her their names.

'Lupus, he's the wolfhound ... Trotter is the terrier ... and Flipper is the pointer ... don't know where Brutus and Ginger are. In the old days they were all over the house, but Lady T doesn't encourage that ... hairs on the satin chairs ... not like the old days ...'

As they walked down the avenue to the kitchen gardens, McDyer pushing his barrow before him, she asked him, 'Do you come up to the kitchen every morning?'

'Every morning. Load up the barrow with what's ordered and walk up the half mile. Every morning. Then in the afternoon, the fruit is sent up. Usually, one of the bothy boys does it — I'm getting a bit old for all this exercise — but they're all away the day.'

'Why don't you send vegetables and fruit up together?'

'Now, Lucy, it's plain you don't know much about gardening. Vegetables are picked in the morning so that they'll be crisp and fresh. Fruit in the afternoon when the sun has warmed it.'

When they reached the walled kitchen garden, McDyer pushed open the gate and they entered. The dogs were left outside. He led the way over to a patch where the cabbages grew.

'Why do you need such high walls?' asked Lucy. 'Is it to keep people out?'

'No, young Lucy. The walls are to protect the fruit-trees and vegetables. This is the south wall — one of the longer ones. Gets the sun early and the red brick warms up during the day so that it's almost like a hot-house.'

'Is that where you grow the peaches?' asked Lucy.

'No, we put them, the nectarines and grapes in the glass-houses. Apples and pears go along the walls. So we get early crops from the south wall ... and later ones from the north wall. That way we can keep the fruit coming for a very long time. Same with the vegetables ...'

'How clever!' said Lucy.

'Common sense. Don't want everything cropping at the same time, do we? Glut today, nothing on the table tomorrow ... now, here are your cabbages. I'll get you a basket...'

When he came out again, he gave her a pear. 'Now, I'm going to give you one of the rarest treats you'll ever have. A Comice pear.

Carrying her basket, with the dogs at her heels, Lucy bit into the luscious sweet pear. 'How self-sufficient they were in those days,' she thought. 'But of course they had to be. Imagine Mrs O'Shea screaming for plums and pears and artichokes ... and nothing available ...

When she came back up the avenue towards the house, she heard the stable clock strike the half hour. It was half past eleven. She had plenty of time. Shooing away the dogs, she slipped into the walled gardens and concealed her basket of cabbage in the high borders. Then she cautiously made her way over to the side which had the ornamental lion's head fountain set into the wall. Luckily, due to the shelter of the walls, the herbaceous border was high and thick, the great clumps of michaelmas daisies still offering shelter.

The air was chilly though the sun was shining, and Lucy was glad when she saw Patrick appearing through the green door. Shortly afterwards, Spencer appeared, in a flurry of movement. For a panic-stricken moment Lucy thought they were going to have their conversation in the open, but Spencer evidently decided that the seat offered a certain amount of concealment and led the way there.

'I haven't long,' she said. 'Her Ladyship is away to lunch with the guns but Mrs Morris wants to see me about something.'

'The house party ends tomorrow,' said Patrick in an irritable

voice. 'Maybe her Ladyship will take it into her head to spend a few days up with the Gordons — and take the ring with her. I knew we left it too late. I should have been away from here long before this.'

'Look, Patrick, I've made up my mind to take the ring. I mentioned to Lady Tyrconnell last night that I saw that girl Lucy skulking around the place — so if it disappears, she's the first suspect.'

'When will you take it?'

'You'll have to leave that to me. But I am resolved now, and I'll give it to you tomorrow night.'

'Took you long enough to make up your mind,' grumbled Patrick.

'It's only that she trusts me. I've never taken as much as a handkerchief from her ... and I still hate doing it now.'

'But it doesn't belong to her. That spoiled brat of a daughter of hers found it. So why shouldn't we have it to start a new life?'

It occurred to Lucy that perhaps Patrick had wanted Spencer

to steal a lot of the Tyrconnell jewellery but Spencer had refused.

'That's another thing, Patrick. Can I trust you this time? After all your flowery talk, you went away before and I didn't hear from you for months ... now you turn up out of the blue and expect me to steal things for you.'

'You know why? I was trying to do better ... to make enough money so that we could get married. I was really only thinking of you, Bessie. I want to give you a good life ...'

'When I take the ring and give it to you, what happens then?'

'Don't you worry about that. I'll disappear again — no one will think anything of that, especially with the house party ending. I'll take the ring to Dublin — I have a few friends in the business there — and sell it. Then I'll send for you.'

'Oh, Patrick, can we not both go away together?'

'No. Her Ladyship would immediately suspect you if you left, and send someone after us. No, you must stay.'

'Don't believe him, Bessie,' Lucy begged silently. 'Can't you see you'll never see him or the ring again.' But the besotted Spencer only said, 'I suppose you know best, Patrick. Now I'd best be getting back.'

'Right. I'll meet you in the coachhouse tomorrow evening. Six sharp. I'll wait for you in the old carriage. It'll be just like old times, Bessie, eh?'

Spencer rose to her feet and hurried off. Patrick yawned and stretched his legs. Lucy hoped that he wasn't going to stay there all day. But then he gave a shiver as the autumn wind blew about him and he sauntered away.

Lucy gave them a good ten minutes before leaving the garden herself.

'Where were you?' asked Nellie curiously, as Lucy slid in beside her in the servants' hall. The upper servants had departed and the others were eating Nesselrode pudding, which had been one of the display pieces the previous evening. 'I've saved a bit of the game pie for you — I have it here.'

Lucy was glad that Mrs O'Shea asked no questions.

'Are the children back yet?' asked Florrie.

'No,' said Mrs O'Shea. 'I understand they won't be back for a few days.'

'Now what am I going to do?' thought Lucy in horror. 'The ring will be stolen tomorrow. I'll be blamed and be sent away before Robert gets back. What on earth am I to do?'

She had almost worked out a desperate plan to try and get up to Glenrea to tell Robert what had happened, but when she got to the nursery, Miss Wade set her mind at rest.

'Well, Lucy, we'll have Miss Elizabeth and Master Robert back tomorrow — they'll be here early as they have to say their good-byes to the house party.'

Lucy was so relieved that she didn't mind another afternoon in the laundry. This time she was at the mangle and very hard work it was, passing folded sheets through so that the water ran out into wooden tubs placed underneath. Then she had to hang them carefully over a wooden rack with small wheels, which she pushed along rails set into the floor and into the drying-room. Then back with the rack to start again.

The next morning Lucy had some sewing to do in the nursery. As she sat sewing away, Miss Wade reading a book by the fire, her only thought was of Robert. When was he going to get back? 'Hurry, hurry,' she begged silently, afraid that at any moment Lady Tyrconnell would sweep into the room and accuse her of stealing the ring. The guests were due to leave about twelve, so surely the children must be back before that. Probably in the fuss and confusion of the departures, Spencer would find an ideal opportunity to take the ring, knowing that if Lady Tyrconnell missed it she could take immediate action, unhampered by the presence of guests.

Was that the sound of hooves in the stable yard? In the

sitting-room it was impossible to tell. But surely there were footsteps in the corridor outside? A moment later Robert burst into the room. Miss Wade looked up, smiling at his impetuosity.

'Really, Robert . . .'

'Guess what, Miss Wade . . . Lucy . . . Parnell won 86 seats! We heard the result this morning.'

Lucy dropped her sewing and Robert gave her a big beam.

'But who won the election?' said a bewildered Miss Wade. 'The Irish Party is only a small one. What about the Conservatives? The Liberals? Who's going to form the Government?'

'Don't know,' said Robert cheerfully. 'That's all I remember. Frederick said that Parnell now held the balance of power.'

'Well, we'll have to wait for the *Freeman's Journal* to arrive to get at the heart of the matter. Really, Robert, if someone gives you information — information, incidentally, of vital importance to all our futures — I hope you'll take it in a little more carefully. Now, children, I think we should go downstairs. The guests will be leaving at noon and we must make our farewells.'

As the governess and children left the room, Lucy cast a look of agony at Robert. A few minutes later he returned and said, 'Anything wrong? Hurry . . . I said I'd forgotten a clean handkerchief and had to go back for it.'

'Spencer is going to steal the ring . . . and give it to Patrick tonight . . . they're going to meet in the coachhouse at six. Then he'll disappear with the ring . . . Oh, Robert, what are we going to do . . . .?'

'This evening? We'll think of something, Lucy. I told Elizabeth, by the way, and she'll help us. You mustn't worry.'

'But, Robert . . . the worst part of it is that Spencer told Lady Tyrconnell that I was seen snooping around the bedrooms . . . and your mother will accuse me of stealing it.'

'Look, we'll work out something. Can you meet Elizabeth and me just after lunch? Frederick gave us a few rare cuttings.

I'll say we must take them down to McDyer,' and he was gone in a flash.

As the clock in the stable yard chimed twelve, Lucy leaned out of the window. Down below on the wide sweep of gravel, carriages were lined up. Grooms sat on the boxes or stood at the head of their pair of horses, and ladies' maids and valets fussed around with small boxes for the luggage carriages. McGinley and Patrick were carrying out trunks and cases.

'Travel light,' thought Lucy. But of course how could they? One ballgown alone would take an entire trunk. And then they had so many changes of costume — last night Mrs O'Shea had told them just how many. 'A morning dress for breakfast, then a tweed suit for the shooting party. An afternoon gown for tea. An evening dress for dinner. And, of course, nightdresses and negligées. And,' Mrs O'Shea had finished off, 'a lady at a house party is supposed never to wear the same dress twice. Why, I heard a story from Lord Iveagh's valet about the lady who wore the same dress on two successive evenings at a house party at the Viceregal Lodge for the Prince of Wales. "Madam," he said to her, "haven't I seen that dress before?" The poor woman was mortified — and properly so — no good being a lady if you don't live up to it.'

Lucy now saw the guests coming out, dressed in travelling suits, hats with veils to protect them from any dust, and fur tippets and muffs. As Lucy watched the good-byes, the fond embraces, the handshakings, she noticed that the men had gathered in a group and were having an animated discussion. 'About Parnell and the Irish Party,' she surmised, in amusement. 'Well, it's the end of the autumn, the end of the house party . . . and in a way the end of an era . . .'

She slowly made her way down to the servants' hall.

'Late again, Lucy,' said Mrs O'Shea. 'Never met such a dawdler in all my life . . . So they're all gone. As I always say, "Never a gathering but a scattering." '

Lucy said nothing. 'What's for dinner?' she asked.

'Game pie,' said Nellie. 'I'm glad the shooting party is over — I've had game up to here. I'll be glad to get back to a bit of good old plain mutton.'

Lucy thought of all the game birds piled high in the shooting brakes. Mallards with their shiny green-blue feathers. The magnificent plumage of the pheasants. The reddish-brown of the grouse. The white-breasted snipe and the dark wings of the woodcock. How sad it was to see their eyes dulled in death. And yet, they would die anyway. Everyone would die. It suddenly occurred to her that when she got back to her own world, Robert and Elizabeth and everyone in that household would be dead.

It was a sobering thought.

## 12 Counterplots

As Lucy was removing the luncheon trays, Robert said to Miss Wade, 'We got some rare cuttings over at Glenrea ... may Elizabeth and I go down to McDyer with them ...?'

'Yes, that will suit nicely. Mrs Morris has asked me to give her a hand rearranging the guest rooms, now that the visitors have all gone.'

'Can I go with them?' asked Lucy. 'Mrs O'Shea asked me to bring back some fruit from the gardens.'

As the children walked along the winding driveway that led to the walled vegetable and fruit garden, Robert was the first to speak.

'Lucy, I'm going to tell mother about your overhearing Patrick telling Spencer to steal the ring.'

'That's no use, she'll never believe it. If Spencer hasn't taken the ring by now, your mother will only lock it up securely — and I'll never get it. If she *has*, I'm going to be accused of stealing it. No, our only chance is to get it before Spencer gives it to Patrick.'

'My father would probably listen to our story,' said Elizabeth. 'Why don't we tell him? He could arrange to be there tonight and get the ring before it's passed over.'

'That's no use either,' said Lucy gloomily. 'If *he* gets the ring, it's still going to be locked away and I'll never get it — don't forget your mother is always going to suspect I'm trying to steal it after what Spencer told her ... Oh, Robert and Elizabeth, I wish with all my heart and soul that I could get that ring. I can't wait any longer. I'm so homesick. It's been nice here and I've enjoyed most of it but I want to see

164

my family again . . .' Overcome, she burst into tears.

'Don't worry, Lucy.' Elizabeth put a comforting arm around her shoulders. 'She's right, Robert. We'll have to get the ring ourselves.'

They sat down on a little bank and thought in silence.

'I know,' said Robert in excitement. 'I could pretend to be Patrick and meet Spencer in the coach-house.'

'But Patrick would arrive at the same time as you . . . and you would be no match for him if it came to a fight.'

'What if we sent a message to Patrick that Spencer couldn't meet him until later,' suggested Elizabeth eagerly.

'We could.' Lucy's heart suddenly rose. 'But where is he staying?'

'He always stays with Jim at the gatehouse when he's here — truth to tell, I don't think Mamma trusts him in the house!' grinned Robert.

'But your voice, Robert? Spencer would know right away that you're not Patrick.' Lucy spirits sank again.

'I'll use my scarf. Wear it round my mouth and pretend I've got a cold. I would wear a hard hat like he does — McGinley would get me one — and a large coat. I'm tall for my age and Patrick is rather small. And remember I'll be sitting in the carriage.'

'I'd forgotten that. Patrick said he would wait in the old man's carriage. Which one is that?' They had seen over the coachhouse one day but all she could remember was that it was full of coaches and carriages of all kinds.

'Grandfather's carriage — it's away at the back of the coach-house,' explained Elizabeth.

'Another thing that will be on our side; it will be getting dark and I'm sure Spencer won't bring a lantern. She would be afraid of Fielding coming out to investigate.'

'I think you're right.' Lucy felt elated again. 'It just might work. Now who does what?'

'I'll talk to McGinley and he'll get me the hat and coat.

I'll go to the coachhouse about a quarter to six — just in case Spencer is early.'

'And I'll slip out to the gatehouse and tell Patrick that Spencer has been delayed by your mother, and not to meet him until tomorrow.'

As they resumed their walk to McDyer, they went over and over all the details of the plan.

'Don't talk much,' was Lucy's final piece of advice. 'Patrick doesn't. Remember, he would be so anxious to get the ring that he would have no time for small talk. Just keep saying, "Give me the ring," and "Hurry, I think Fielding's coming."'

Under normal circumstances, Lucy would have enjoyed the visit to McDyer. This time, as he talked about crops and stores and seeds and plants and planting, the children visibly showed their impatience. But old McDyer appeared not to notice.

'Grapes, you want, Lucy? Come into the store and you can get yourself some of the finest bunches I've ever grown.'

They followed him into a cool dark store which was lined with racks. In each circular hole, stored at a slant, was a bottle which held a bunch of grapes on a stalk.

'Rainwater and charcoal — that's what keeps them fresh. Up to 300 bunches here and they'll last until next May. By that time we'll be cutting the new grapes ... now what about pears ... the Comice are magnificent ...' and he brought them to another store which had shelves covered with pears. He selected a few for Lucy's basket.

'Now, can I show you over the gardens?' he offered.

Lucy cast an anxious look at Robert, but he was already saying, 'It's very kind of you, McDyer, and Elizabeth and I would love to see them some other time. Perhaps tomorrow. But Mamma wants to see us at teatime and we mustn't be late.'

'Neither must you. Well, off with you, and you, Lucy, tell Mrs O'Shea she must come down herself and see what's in stock. Give her a few ideas.' He said, almost to himself, 'Off you go then, but never forget I run the most important part of the gardens. Did you ever hear the old rhyme?'

They had to pause to listen as he recited:

> *I cannot eat the red, red rose,*
> *I cannot eat the white.*
> *In vain the long laburnum glows,*
> *Vain the camellia's waxen snows,*
> *The lily's cream of light.*
> *The lilac's clustered chalices*
> *Proffer their bounty sweet*
> *In vain! Though very good for bees,*
> *Man, with unstinted yearning sees,*
> *Admires but cannot eat.*

'You remember that, young people. Fruit and vegetables beat flowers hands down any day.'

'I thought he was never going to stop,' laughed Elizabeth as they skipped back home. 'I'll go straight to Mamma's room and get the ring if it's there; if it's gone, I'll bring you word ... Robert, you'll have to see McGinley straightway and, Lucy, you make sure you get down to the gatelodge at five-thirty. See you in the schoolroom.'

Lucy went into the kitchen to show her basket to Mrs O'Shea, happily singing, 'I cannot eat the red, red rose,' but the cook cut her short. 'Her Ladyship wants to see you in the nursery. On the double. So go ... and try and get back as soon as possible. You mustn't think that because the guests are gone there's no work to be done. Staff always expect an extra special dinner the first night after they go. So hurry.'

When Lucy got to the sitting-room, Lady Tyrconnell was already there. She was standing at the table, hands clasped in front of her. Her blue eyes were glittering coldly.

Elizabeth stood behind her and when Lucy came in, she pointed to her ring finger and shook her head. So Spencer had stolen the ring!

Miss Wade and Robert, both looking unhappy, were also in the room and Lucy guessed Lady Tyrconnell had already told them about the theft.

'What have you done with it?' she asked in a measured, hostile voice.

'D ... done ... done with what?' stammered Lucy.

'The ruby ring, you odious child.' Lady Tyrconnell's voice rose.

'I haven't got it.' Lucy was surprised at how firm and steady her voice sounded.

'So you intend to deny the theft. Very well! Miss Wade, take Lucy to your room. I want her thoroughly searched.'

As Lucy was led away in disgrace, Robert flashed her a comforting glance. In Miss Wade's bedroom, the governess said, 'I am sorry things should come to this pass, Lucy. I thought you were a bright girl and would turn out to be a responsible servant. It seems I was mistaken about you. Your aunt will be bitterly disappointed. Undress now, please, stockings and boots as well.'

As Lucy stood shivering in her long petticoats, the governess carefully examined the pockets in the discarded dress and apron. Then she turned the ugly boots upside down and shook them. She was examining the thick black stockings when the voice of Lady Tyrconnell spoke from the doorway.

'Has she the ring concealed on her person?'

'No, your Ladyship.' Miss Wade was running her hands over the petticoats, feeling every inch of Lucy's body.

'Strip searching,' thought Lucy in anger, though she could hardly blame Miss Wade.

Lady Tyrconnell was speaking again. 'I will not be made a fool of by this sly baggage. Before she is sent away, I want that ring found ...'

Lucy gasped in horror. When would she be sent away?

'... Her room must be searched. If it isn't there, then all the servants must be questioned. Someone may know where she has hidden it. The scullery-maid, the one she shares a room with. She may know something. Now, Miss Wade, come with me and we'll draw up a list of the servants we want to see ... Elizabeth, Robert, you may take tea with me.'

When Lucy had dressed herself and been led back into the sitting-room, Lady Tyrconnell said coldly, before she swept out of the room, 'This girl is to have no contact with my children. Lock her into the brush room. When we complete our investigations, I will decide when she is to be sent back to her aunt. Children, you are not to come up to the nursery again until she is gone.'

As Robert passed her, in the wake of his mother, he made a pressing motion with his hand. Lucy was puzzled; then suddenly she realised he was telling her not to forget to open the panel to the secret stairs.

When they were alone, Miss Wade asked her in a rather softer voice, 'Did you take the ring, Lucy? If you tell me, and it is returned to Lady Tyrconnell, perhaps we can make some other arrangement for you. You obviously can't stay here but I might be able to help you. Do tell the truth, Lucy?'

'I *am* telling the truth, Miss Wade. I didn't take it,' said Lucy miserably.

'Oh, Lucy, I wish I could believe you. I do hope there may be some other explanation for its disappearance . . . perhaps Spencer misplaced it.'

'I wouldn't exactly say "misplaced",' thought Lucy. 'I'm sure it's now in a very good place indeed.'

Miss Wade brought her to the brush room, and before she locked her in she said, 'I'll get someone to bring you some supper — *if* you give me your word of honour that you won't try to escape.'

Lucy promised, reflecting that, theft or no theft, Miss Wade thought her word of honour could be trusted!

As she heard the key turning in the lock, she sat down on the small stool and reviewed her position. It could hardly be worse. Spencer had the ring and she would pass it over to Patrick. He would disappear off to Dublin, sell it, and that would be the end of that. She would be a prisoner in 1885 forever. And where would she go? Langley Castle was lost to her and this so-called aunt would disown her and put her in an orphanage or in the workhouse.

She tried to think cheerfully of Elizabeth and Robert. Maybe their plan would succeed. She could trust Robert to do his part, but who would take the message to Patrick in the gatelodge? She could hardly see Elizabeth in the role of messenger. Perhaps they would send McGinley or Nellie. But probably all the servants would be required to stay indoors for questioning. No, the plan was doomed to failure. From depression, her mood changed to anger at herself. Why hadn't she made greater efforts to get the ring when she knew where it was? It would only have taken a few minutes to make her second wish, and yet she had fumbled her chance when she was in Lady Tyrconnell's bedroom. She should have stayed in the dressing-room and taken the ring, instead of worrying about being detected. However, there was no use crying over lost chances, she thought, beginning to cry again.

The stillness was broken by the sound of the key being turned in the lock. Lucy tensed, her eyes on the door. Was Miss Wade coming back to tell her she must go now? But, no, it was Minnie, who said in an exasperated voice, 'As if I didn't have enough work!' She banged down a plate with a few slices of bread and butter. 'They're fairly talking about you downstairs, young Lucy. Imagine stealing a ring belonging to her Ladyship. Even Nellie is lost for words.'

'Oh, Minnie,' said poor Lucy. 'I didn't take it. I swear I didn't.'

'Well, I hope it turns up — mind you, it wouldn't be the first time her Ladyship has mislaid something and tried to blame one of the servants.'

'Do tell them in the kitchen I'm innocent. I couldn't bear it if they thought I was a thief.'

'I will. Except for Winters,' here Minnie giggled. 'He says he knew from the moment he set eyes on you that there was something peculiar about you. And he says he's never wrong about people . . . now, if you're finished, I'll take the plate. See you at supper-time. Don't worry — I'm sure it will all come right.'

When she had gone, relocking the door behind her, Lucy thought grimly, 'Well, old Winters isn't such a dope after all . . . "something peculiar" indeed!'

As daylight began to fade the brush room became even darker. Lucy tried to figure out what time it was but that was impossible. Was it half past five yet? Or six o'clock, the time for the meeting? Had Robert and Elizabeth managed to get anyone to take the message to the gatelodge? But Nellie was in the kitchen when Minnie was getting the food for Lucy. It couldn't be her. Perhaps McGilney had gone . . . She sat down beside the panel with the knob and pressed it, hearing again the familiar click. Somehow it was the only thing that could comfort her now.

She must have dozed briefly but a sudden noise jolted her into wakefulness. Her heart gave a joyful leap when Elizabeth climbed through the secret entrance. She threw her arms around Lucy. 'So far, so good!'

'What happened? What happened?' cried Lucy.

'We got the message to Patrick. At least,' proudly, 'I did.'

'You did?' Lucy was dumbfounded.

'When we finished tea, Robert said we wanted to go and see the ponies. On the way to the stables, we talked it over and decided to get McGinley to go down with the message — we can always trust him. But we couldn't find him. Mamma had made all the servants assemble in the servants' hall — really she fusses terribly sometimes, doesn't she? We didn't know what to do ... and then I said, "*I'll* do it. Surely I'm capable of a small thing like that?"'

'So I put on my coat and ran down the avenue. Patrick was in the gatehouse and I said to him that I had a message for him from Spencer — that she had hurt her ankle and couldn't walk, and wanted to meet him tomorrow night instead. Same time. Same place.'

'What did he say?'

'He looked surprised to see me, but I explained that I was there when she slipped, and that she asked me, as a great favour, to carry the message to him. Mind you, he was wary enough to ask why one of the servants hadn't brought the message but I explained that there was some trouble — I didn't know what — and Mamma had asked all the servants to assemble in the servants' hall. That fairly took the wind out of his sails! So off I ran. I'm pretty sure he won't go anywhere near the coachhouse tonight — or any other night for that matter. He probably figures the game is up.'

'You're marvellous,' said Lucy, admiration in her voice. 'I wouldn't have been as smart as you.'

'Now,' said Elizabeth settling herself on the floor, oblivious of her dress. 'All we have to do is to wait until Robert comes

back. So, cross your heart, Lucy. Are you any good at praying?'

'Sometimes,' admitted Lucy, thinking of the night of the short prayers.

As they sat there in the gloom, the spluttering candle throwing strange shadows on the wall, Elizabeth said suddenly, 'I meant to tell you about that morning that you made me go down to meet Frederick.'

'I didn't exactly *make* you,' Lucy smiled.

'Well, only for you I wouldn't have gone down. And only for you I wouldn't have behaved so well. I would have been showing off as usual, trying to be better than anyone else. I just relaxed and we had a very pleasant time. And between that morning and the visit to Glenrea, I really got to know Frederick better ... he said so. When we were riding back to Langley yesterday — Robert was behind with Fielding — he told me he had been in despair, that I was always snubbing him and that he was sure I didn't like him at all ... Lucy, marriage or no marriage, I think we'll always be great friends. I know now I can talk to him about anything.'

'I'm so glad,' replied Lucy.

Elizabeth threw back her head, and hugging her knees more tightly said, 'Lucy, what makes you so wise? Why do you understand me so well? How did you know that I wanted to meet Frederick that morning, but having made such a fuss, I was determined to pretend I didn't?'

Lucy smiled again. 'I used to know someone like you once. She really meant very well, but if she didn't get everything she wanted — and if she wasn't always first — she flew into a tantrum and made everyone else miserable. Her poor brother was always trying to please her ... and she just walked on him.'

'What became of her?'

'I think she learned not to worry about things that didn't matter and appreciate those that did. In short, she grew up.'

They both laughed.

Then they heard the sound they had been waiting for. The sound of someone coming up the secret stairs. The panel opened again and Robert came into the room.

'Guess what?'

'You got it, you got it!' yelled Lucy, throwing caution to the winds.

'Yes! I'll tell you all about it ... as soon as I got my breath back.

'You should have seen my outfit,' he laughed. 'McGinley got me an old jacket belonging to one of the odd-jobs men — much like the one Patrick would wear carrying in the coals. And an old hat of his that he stuffed with paper to make it fit. Then I added a scarf and went to the coachhouse.

'I was sitting in the old carriage so long that I thought she wasn't coming. It was rather a strange feeling, being there all on my own, feeling so nervous. Luckily, I think Spencer was even more nervous than I was. Probably on account of all the fuss about the ring and Mamma assembling everyone — she must have had quite a job to get away. She didn't delay at all. She just pushed the box into my hand and rushed away. Wouldn't it be a turn-up if she told Mamma that Patrick had the ring and he was caught red-handed?'

'Not a chance,' said Lucy cheerfully. 'I'll bet he's half way to Dublin by now. He wouldn't want to stay around for any investigation.'

'Lucy,' said Robert in a serious tone of voice, 'before I hand over the ring, can I ask you something?'

'Of course!' Lucy was in jubilant mood. After all the disappointments, all the heart-searchings, all the agony, she had the ring! Home was only a short while away. Then, looking at Robert's troubled face, she asked, 'What is it? Something is troubling you.'

Robert's face was very serious as he spoke. 'Lucy, you come from another age. Elizabeth and I are both convinced of that now. You're over a hundred years away from us. You know everything that happened in that century ... tell me, what happened to people like us? Papa and the others keep saying that there will be no place for them under Home Rule. That the tenants will get the land. That the landlords will be finished. Is that true ...?'

Lucy thought for a moment, wondering what exactly to say. Then she said slowly, 'Ireland didn't get Home Rule in 1885, nor in the years after. The country didn't get free of England until much later. There was the Great War from 1914 to 1918 — Ireland had been promised Home Rule but it was shelved until after that war. But some people didn't wait. There was a Rising in 1916 and a lot of fighting but we separated from England in 1921, except for six counties in the north.'

'Was Donegal one of them?' asked Elizabeth.

'No, it became part of the Republic of Twenty-Six Counties.' She laughed at the sudden thought and said, 'Now if you had lived in County Fermanagh ... I read somewhere that George V insisted that Fermanagh remain part of the United Kingdom — because the Duke of Westminster had estates there and he didn't want to part from England.'

'But I would have wanted to stay Irish — I *am* Irish ... Lucy,' Robert pressed, 'what happened to the landowners? Did the tenants get the right to buy out the land?'

'Yes, there were a lot of Land Acts — I'm a big vague about this. But ...'

'Lucy, you haven't answered the question,' said Robert gently. 'Will we ... will Langley ... still be here a hundred years from now?'

'I'm trying to think of the words of a poem by one of our greatest poets, W.B. Yeats — he would have been born by now :

*I came upon a great house in the middle of the night,*
*Its open lighted doorway and its windows all alight,*
*And all my friends were there and made me welcome too;*
*But I woke in an old ruin that the winds howled through ...*

Some of the landlords went to live in England. Some of the big houses were burned out in the fighting. But many stayed on and became part of the new Ireland. Oh, Robert and Elizabeth, I'm sure your family would have stayed. I'm sure your descendants will still be living here in my day ...'

'You'd better go now, Lucy,' said Elizabeth. 'There's probably a hue and cry on for us now. And Minnie may sneak up with some supper for you ... Won't Miss Wade get a shock when she finds you're gone ...'

'I wish,' said Lucy, 'that there was some way that I could convince everyone that I didn't steal the ring ...'

'We'll think up something,' said Elizabeth. 'We'll tell Mamma that you really did own the ring and that we helped you to get it back when you lost it.'

'*That* would be a miracle,' said Lucy laughing, 'but it's nice of you to try .. .I'm going to miss you both very much.'

'I know,' said Elizabeth. 'I just wish you could stay on.'

'Langley won't be the same without you.' There was a sadness in Robert's voice that cut Lucy to the heart.

'If we promise never to forget each other, that would help a little, wouldn't it?' asked Lucy.

The other two agreed and in the shadowy room that would hold so many memories for ever, the three friends solemnly shook hands, and promised to remember each other always, even though time would separate them henceforth.

Robert took the ring from the box and handed it to Lucy.

'I have to wear it on my right hand for the magic to work,' explained Lucy. 'There was a rhyme written inside the original box ...'

'Can you remember the rhyme, Lucy?' asked Elizabeth.

Placing the ring on her right hand, she recited:

> *The secret of this Ruby Ring,*
> *Is that two wishes it can bring,*
> *On right hand, middle finger place,*
> *And turn the ring around but twice.*
> *Now, make your wish, then wait and see ...*
> *How magic the Ruby Ring can be ...*

'There is someone coming,' Robert said urgently.

Lucy rapidly turned the ruby ring twice and said fervently, 'I wish to be back in my home again.'

'Good-bye, Elizabeth. Good-bye, Robert. I'll never forget you. Say good-bye to Nellie for me.'

Lucy's eyelids were already drooping and the peculiar floating sensation was returning. Her stomach was beginning to churn and the voices of Elizabeth and Robert calling good-byes were getting fainter and fainter. She heard the faint click as they opened the secret panel and then there was nothing ...

## 13   The Past Remembered

The next thing Lucy felt was someone gently shaking her by the shoulder, saying, 'Lucy, Lucy, it's late. Wake up.'

'Oh, Nellie, I mustn't be late today or Miss Wade will be angry,' Lucy said in panic, as she sat bolt upright in bed.

By now her eyes were wide open and she blinked in delighted amazement when she saw that it was her mother who was standing by her bed.

'It's really you, Mum! It's really you! I just can't believe it!' she said with a sigh of relief. 'You're not angry with me, are you? Did you wonder what had happened to me?'

'Well, when you called me Nellie, I knew exactly what had happened to you,' said her mother with a smile. 'You have been dreaming again.'

'No, no, it wasn't a dream. I've been away for ages and I was getting scared that I would never see you again ... It's all because of the ruby ring. It's magic. There was a message printed inside the bottom of the box. Wait, I'll show you,' Lucy reached eagerly for the box on the bedside table. 'There's a secret hinge, and the bottom lifts up,' she explained as she tried to find it. Nothing happened. 'That's strange. It worked the Friday night I got the ring. Wait, I'll just tell you the message. It said ... it said ... oh, no ... I can't remember.' Her voice was full of consternation.

Mrs McLaughlin sat on the edge of the bed and hugged her. 'Lucy, darling. Last night was Friday night — the night you got the ring. I think that getting it over-excited you and that you dreamt that the ring was magic. Some dreams are so real that when you wake up you think they really happened.

178

But's it's all over now and you'll soon forget it. Remember, it's Saturday and we must go and choose your present today.' Drawing back the curtains, she continued, 'It's a lovely autumn day, so we'll be able to shop in comfort. I hate it when it's raining. Everyone with their umbrellas bumping into each other, and getting grumpy and bad-tempered ... Now, hurry up and get dressed. The others have already started breakfast.'

When her mother left the room, Lucy lay back and gazed around at all her familiar possessions. Everything was just as she remembered it. Could her mother be right? Was it all just a dream? But she could remember so clearly everything that had happened. Her panic when she discovered the ring was missing. All the times she had tried to get it back. Surely she couldn't have dreamt up Robert, or Elizabeth, who had been so nasty to her in the beginning. And Nellie and her sad story — she couldn't have dreamt that too. And Miss Wade the governess and Mrs O'Shea and Winters who didn't like her and McGinley who was so nice. And all the hard work and the long dresses and aprons and caps and the ugly brown dress she had worn at first. Surely it wasn't all just a dream. Had not she and Robert and Elizabeth shaken hands and promised never to forget one another?

Gazing down, Lucy saw she was wearing her own nightdress and the ruby ring glowed reassuringly from her right hand.

'Oh, well,' she thought with a sigh. 'I'm glad it's all over. It was rather scarey at times. Robert and Elizabeth were the best part ... I won't ever forget them.'

As these thoughts were running through her mind she was hastily donning jeans and sweatshirt, and brushing her teeth quickly she raced downstairs to the kitchen.

Sitting down she helped herself to a large plate of cornflakes. 'Mmmm,' she said, 'I really missed my cornflakes.'

'Lucy,' said her mother with a laugh. 'You had cornflakes yesterday morning.'

'Did I? I'd forgotten,' and as she ate hungrily she asked,

'Are you going to make porridge this winter, Mum?'

'Why?' Mrs McLaughlin was bewildered. 'But you never take it anyway.'

'Well, I may from now on,' Lucy informed the surprised table.

'Did you sleep well last night, Lucy?' Grannie McLaughlin asked as she poured another cup of tea.

'Funny, you should ask, Gran, because I feel as if I haven't slept at all. I had the strangest dream ever.'

'Did you indeed?' Gran sounded thoughtful. 'You know that dreams can sometimes change a person's life.'

'That's right, Gran. I feel like a different person this morning.'

David, who had finished his breakfast, said, 'Mum, I'm going upstairs to play with Ultra Magnus.'

'Would you like to take my Lego?' said Lucy.

David stopped in his tracks. 'Is this some sort of trick, Lucy?' he asked uncertainly.

'No, David, I'm getting too old for Lego now, so you may have it.'

'To keep?' asked David in amazement.

'To keep, forever and a day,' said Lucy cheerfully.

'Gosh, thanks a million, Lucy. It will be smashing to put it all together with my own,' David said as he dashed off happily.

During this conversation, Jean and Paul exchanged raised eyebrows. Was this the Lucy who guarded her possessions with a ferocity that had worried them both in the past?

Finishing breakfast, Lucy asked, 'Could I go and see Noreen, Mum? It's urgent. I'll tidy my room when I get back.'

'All right,' said her mother with an understanding smile, and with her father's warning of 'Be careful crossing the road,' Lucy ran off. Going up Main Street she couldn't resist having a quick look into the window of Gallaghers which was the biggest toy shop in the town. Jigsaws, books, radios, dolls, games, and records were all crowded into the windows. 'It's going to be hard to make a choice,' she thought to herself. 'Suppose I'd better find out what Mum and Dad can afford first.'

She dragged herself away from the window and continued on to the back road where the Dohertys lived. Her footsteps slowed as she approached number 47, and with heart wildly beating she wondered if she was wise in calling. Noreen had said she would never speak to her again. 'Well, I'll just have to take it on the chin if she won't speak to me . . . but I've got to try.' Squaring her shoulders and taking a deep breath, she rang the bell.

The door was opened by Mrs Doherty. 'Is . . . is Noreen in?' stammered Lucy.

'She is indeed, Lucy,' said Mrs Doherty. 'She's upstairs hoovering the rooms, so I'm sure she'll be glad to escape for a while. Go into the sitting-room and I'll call her.'

Lucy waited apprehensively, wondering what she would say if Mrs Doherty came down and said, 'She doesn't want to see you.' But very shortly the door opened and an unsmiling Noreen came in.

Lucy rushed into speech before her courage could fail her. 'Noreen, I want to apologise. I know it was rotten of me to tell your secret. What I did was unforgiveable and I'll quite understand if you never want to speak to me again. I'm afraid,' she hesitated before she continued, 'I'm afraid I was jealous of you because you are more popular than I am. And then when I didn't win the essay prize, I felt I just had nothing . . . Will you forgive me?'

Noreen's face still had that sad look. 'I was very upset about it, Lucy. I didn't want everyone jeering me and saying I was a fool to want to be a writer . . . and the fact that it was you, my best friend, who told everyone . . . that made it worse . . .'

'Nobody is going to jeer you, Noreen,' said Lucy. 'You're much too nice. They'll jeer me of course, and I deserve it. So can we be friends again?'

Noreen smiled at last. 'Of course. I don't know what I would do without you, Lucy. We've been friends for such ages . . . I wouldn't know what to do if you made best-friends with someone else.'

'Great . . . now you're coming to my party, aren't you?'

'I'm looking forward to it. Three o'clock tomorrow, isn't it? And I've got a little present for you, but I won't give it to you until tomorrow.'

'I'll just have to be patient until then . . . but see,' she stretched out her hand, 'I've got one present already.'

'It's just fabulous,' gasped Noreen. 'Can I try it on?'

Lucy handed it over, then said urgently, 'Don't put it on your right hand, Noreen.'

'Why not?' Noreen asked in surprise.

'I'm . . . I'm not quite sure. I seem to have forgotten. Something about the right hand, when you put it on for the first time.'

'I'll try it on my left hand,' said Noreen, putting it on and admiring the rich glow of the star cut ruby. 'It's very beautiful.'

'Mum is going to lock it away for me until I'm older,' said Lucy.

At the front door, she turned awkwardly and said, 'Noreen, I'm genuinely glad you won the essay competition and I'm looking forward to hearing it read out on Monday. Who knows? Maybe we'll both be writers some day.'

Noreen beamed and then said with a mischievous grin, 'By the way the essay is called "My Best Friend" — so you should like it.'


When lunch was over the McLaughlin family and Gran all piled into the car. Paul had promised a special outing to a big house called Dunard.

On the way, Lucy asked, 'Do you think I could go to an Irish college, next summer?'

'I'd be all for it,' said her father. 'But I didn't think you were all that interested in Irish.'

'I want to take more of an interest from now on. As they say: *Tir gan teanga, Tir gan ainm.*'

'You're full of surprises today, Lucy,' said her mother as the car passed Lough Eske and entered Barnesmore Gap, with its high bald mountains rising on either side. They looked at Biddy's of Barnes, a pub which had served the travellers passing through the gap since 1805.

As they went through the forest outside Ballybofey, Lucy had already nodded off, her head resting on Gran's shoulder.

'Wake up, Lucy, we're here,' Gran was saying as she gently nudged Lucy awake. Lucy yawned and stretched and was quite wide awake by the time they reached the avenue with its great gates and the circular globes on top of the pillars, and drove up the wide driveway. It was edged with shrubs and beyond were great trees, vivid in their autumn colouring.

'If we hurry, we can get on the three o'clock tour,' Dad was saying as he parked the car around the side of the house. As she got out, Lucy gasped. 'It can't be!' But it was. The walled garden of her dream, exactly as she remembered it.

As they turned towards the house, a further shock awaited her. A wide flight of stone steps led to the front door of the large square house — just like Langley Castle, except that it was now covered in ivy.

But her father had called it Dunard Castle. 'Did all big houses look alike then?' she wondered. Now they were in the great entrance hall, with its marble floor, the tall columns supporting the high ceiling and the wide staircase leading up to the first landing.

'The guide has just started,' said the receptionist. 'If you go in to your left, you'll be able to join the group.'

'This is the drawing-room,' the guide was explaining. 'The furniture is French and very fine. It was all brought to Langley, as Dunard Castle was known then, by the Lady Tyrconnell who had the house built. There was another house on the site before that — the Tyrconnells have lived here since the 1600s, they were a branch of the Red Hugh O'Donnell family — but Lady Tyrconnell, who was English, decided to rebuild the main part of the castle which had fallen into very bad repair.'

Lucy had eyes for only one piece of furniture in the room. It was the black lacquered cabinet, so beautifully inlaid with flowers and birds. It still stood in front of the secret panel.

The guide was speaking again. 'These fine paintings are of a previous owner, the grandfather of the present Lord Tyrconnell. His name was Robert and the matching portrait is of his sister Elizabeth. They are rather unusual in many ways. It is more usual to have matching portraits of husband and wife — there is a portrait of that Lord Tyrconnell's wife but it's in the morning-room. And, in those days, they usually put family portraits in the dining-room because it was the tradition . . .

'To dine with your ancestors,' Lucy couldn't help putting in mischievously.

The guide smiled at her. 'I can see you've been reading the guide-book.'

Lucy made her way to the front of the group, almost pressing against the rope that divided the room, to get a better view. And there on the wall, in heavy gilt frames, Elizabeth and Robert smiled down on her, older than they had been when she had known them, but unmistakably her two friends.

'What happened to Elizabeth?' she asked.

'She married the Earl of Gordon, when she was sixteen. The portrait was painted at a later stage and I understand that the Earl was very anxious to have it hung at his place, Glenrea Castle. But Robert insisted it remain here, and that both portraits be placed in the drawing room . . . they both seemed to have a special affection for this room.'

'Did she have any children?' asked Lucy, much to the guide's delight; he loved when people took an interest in the house.

'Yes, indeed — she had ten.' Everyone gasped, and he went on, 'Nowadays everyone thinks it was only the very poor who had large families in those days. But, in fact, the aristocracy also had very large families. Now I must tell you an interesting story about Lady Gordon. Her first child was a girl, and she called her ... But, before I tell you that,' a dramatic pause, 'I want to draw your attention to this portrait in the corner. This is a young servant called Lucy, who worked here when these two,' gesturing at the portraits, 'were children in the house. It appears that Elizabeth and Robert, the children of Lord Tyrconnell, became very fond of this girl and they had her portrait painted. Again it was stipulated that it should always remain in the drawing-room. What the connection was, we're not quite sure, but,' triumphantly, 'Elizabeth, the Countess of Gordon, called her first child Lucy. The portrait incidentally, was painted from a sketch that Elizabeth did as a girl.'

Lucy could feel a hysterical giggle rising in her throat as

she looked at the portrait of herself in the long blue dress and apron. How well she remembered the morning Elizabeth had sketched her — and all the commands to stop fidgeting.

'Look, Lucy,' whispered David. 'She's wearing a ring almost like yours. Isn't that odd?'

'Yes indeed,' said Gran. 'What a coincidence. And the girl has red hair.'

The guide, thinking what an intelligent group he had with him today, said, 'I know you'll be interested in this.'

'This' was a small glass-topped display cabinet.

'It contains a letter from another servant, a scullery-maid, I think, who was also in the castle at that time. The Lord Tyrconnell in the portrait helped her to trace her family. Apparently they had been evicted and went to America. She was left behind — it's not quite clear why — and he wrote a letter for her to an address she had been given. And so her family was found and later he got his father to pay her fare to America. Not only that, before she left he arranged for her to learn to read and write — the poor girl could do neither.

'He was apparently a very kind landlord, very good to the tenants, and that was why, during the troubles, Dunard Castle was never touched. Nor was Glenrea Castle.

'By the way, if you visit Glenrea, and I would strongly recommend it, you will see a copy of that portrait,' pointing to the one of Elizabeth, 'there. Her husband commissioned it specially.'

'Some of the landlords were not so good,' said Gran. 'Weren't there some frightful evictions in Donegal?'

'Yes, indeed. Those at Glenveagh were the most notorious. The magnificent castle there was built by the owner, Adair, for his American wife — she was the widow of a colonel of the United States Army. When he died, she had an inscription carved on the face of a large rock perched on a ledge high above Lough Veagh:

*To the memory of John George Adair.*
*Brave, just and generous.*

And now we come to a very strange happening. One night, during a raging storm, a bolt of lightning struck the rock and sent it crashing in bits to the depths of the lake.'

'Mrs O'Shea would have been pleased,' thought Lucy, remembering her solemn epitaph: Black as the Earl of Hell's waistcoat.

By now the next group was appearing in the main doorway, and Lucy's group was led across the hall into the dining-room. Lucy remembered the last time she had seen it, set up for the first grand dinner of the house party — the sparkle of the chandeliers, the gleam of the silver, the flowers and the luscious fruit displays, Winters casting a careful eye over everything, and McGinley checking the table settings. She peeped out through the second door into the hall, thinking of the time that Ethel had given her a glimpse of the party of ladies descending the main stairs to go into the drawing-room.

'Come on, Lucy,' called Gran. 'The guide is taking us down to the kitchens.'

'The kitchens are not in general use now,' explained the guide. 'The present Lord and Lady Tyrconnell use the small kitchen upstairs that was installed by his father. After the first world war, servants became scarce and without the staff to run them, the kitchens became obsolete. Now they are only used if there is a big party upstairs.'

How still and cold and desolate the kitchen quarters were, now that the once always-glowing fire in the range was quenched. Lucy closed her eyes and found the silence unbearable. Where was Mrs O'Shea who should be shouting instructions at Florrie and Maggie, Bella Jane whisking in and out with her trays of scones for afternoon tea, Nellie chopping vegetables, eternally interrupted by shouts of 'number one' or 'number six'? The pots and saucepans were still there on the shelves, but now they were only lifeless objects. They were no longer part of everyday life — they would never be used again.

'The kitchen is kept exactly as it was,' the guide told them.

'What beautiful copper utensils,' said someone.

'Yes, and it takes quite a lot of work to keep them shining like that. Two women come up from the village to make sure they are always in perfect condition.'

'And poor Nellie used to do it all by herself,' thought Lucy. She peeped into the scullery where she and Nellie had faced those mountains of dirty pots and pans, and then into the laundry where the giant mangles stood in lonely isolation. Where was the steam, the heat, the piles of washing, the splashing of water, the voices of Becky and Mary Kate rising over the creaking of the mangles? Now it was all as silent as the grave. The game larder was empty and the doors along the corridor were shut.

Lucy was glad to leave the kitchens; the contrast between all the busy bustle she remembered and the emptiness of now was unbearable.

In the hall upstairs, she asked the guide if she might have another look into the drawing-room to see Nellie's letter. 'You go on,' she said to her family, 'I won't be a moment.'

She took a brief look at the letter. So Nellie had found her family. Things had come all right for her in the end. Lucy wondered if she married. Had she any children? Of course she would have married and would have told the children over and over again the story of the eviction and of her days at Langley Castle.

Then, checking to make sure she was alone, she ducked under the dividing rope and went to the wall behind the cabinet. She remembered how they had wondered if the secret staircase could be opened from the drawing-room. Now she was about to find out! Pressing the carved centre knob, she once again

heard the familiar click and gently easing open the panel, she peered into the murky darkness where everything was still and the cobwebs had taken over once more. Shutting the panel quietly, she murmured with a sigh, 'Good-bye, Elizabeth. Good-bye, Robert. I'll never forget you.'

She ducked back under the rope again and with tears in her eyes she waved to the watching portraits. As she crossed the hall, a tall man was coming down the stairs. Someone called, 'Lord Tyrconnell,' and he smiled at Lucy. This was Robert's grandson. How like him he was. The same eyes, the same kindly smile.

'I hope you enjoyed your visit to Dunard,' he said.

'Oh, indeed I did. It's the nicest place I've ever been in. It must be lovely to live in a big house like this.'

Then, with quickening footsteps, she went to rejoin her family.

## *Acknowledgements*

I would like to thank Maureen McIntyre of Glenties Library for all the help she has given me; also the County Library in Letterkenny.

I read a great many books and newspapers on the Ireland of 1885. Particularly helpful were *Land War and Eviction in Derryveagh* by Liam Dolan (Annaverna Press, Dundalk), and *History of Landlordism in Donegal* by Prionnriar O Gallcobair (Donegal Democrat).

The lines of poetry that Lucy quotes to Robert in Chapter Twelve come from *The Curse of Cromwell* by W.B. Yeats.

The anecdotes of life 'upstairs' come from several sources. The old lady who sent the laconic telegram 'Returning Tuesday kill a sheep', and who married for the third time at the age of eighty was Louisa Jephson-Norreys of Mallow Castle (*An Anglo-Irish Miscellany* by Maurice Denham Jepson).

Yvonne MacGrory
November 1991

Yvonne MacGrory was born in and grew up in County Donegal, in the northwest of Ireland. She is a state registered nurse and lives in the town of Kilraine, County Donegal, with her husband, Eamon, and their three children, Jane, Donna, and Mark. She likes to read, sketch, work in the garden, and solve crossword puzzles. *The Secret of the Ruby Ring* is her first book.

Terry Myler studied at the National College of Art in Dublin, Ireland. She has illustrated many children's books in Ireland, including *The Legend of the Golden Key, Cornelius Rabbit of Tang,* and *The Children of the Forge.* She lives in Wicklow hills, near Dublin, with her husband, daughter, two dogs, and one cat.

*If you enjoyed this book, you will also want to read these other Milkweed novels:*

*Gildaen*
*The Heroic Adventures of a Most Unusual Rabbit*
Emilie Buchwald
Winner of the Chicago Tribune Book Festival Award,
Best Book for Ages 9-12

*I Am Lavina Cumming*
Susan Lowell
Winner of the Mountains & Plains
Booksellers Association Award

*A Bride for Anna's Papa*
Isabel R. Marvin
Milkweed Prize for Children's Literature